Leningrad

Leningrad

Igor Vishnevetsky

Translated by
Andrew Bromfield

DALKEY ARCHIVE PRESS
CHAMPAIGN / LONDON / DUBLIN

Originally published in Russian by Vremia, Moscow, 2012

Library of Congress Cataloging-in-Publication Data

Vishnevetskii, I. G., author.
[Leningrad. English]
Leningrad / Igor Vishnevetsky ; translated by Andrew Bromfield.
pages ; cm
ISBN 978-1-56478-902-0 (alk.: pbk)
1. Saint Petersburg (Russia)--History--Siege, 1941-1944--Fiction. I. Bromfield,
Andrew, translator. II. Title.
PG3489.3.I679L4613 2013
891.73'5--dc23
2013035340

Partially funded by a grant from the Illinois Arts Council, a state agency

Published with the support of the Institute for Literary Translation, Russia

ИНСТИТУТ ПЕРЕВОДА

www.dalkeyarchive.com

Cover: design and composition by Mikhail Iliatov

Printed on permanent/durable acid-free paper

CONTENTS

In loving memory of my father

ESSENTIAL INTRODUCTORY NOTE

Leningrad *is crammed with quotations—*
both verbatim and modified—
which tell the story of events
that took place in reality
or in the imagination.
I have merely arranged them
in a specific order

IGOR VISHNEVETSKY
AUTUMN 2009

PART ONE: AUTUMN

Chapter One
DITHYRAMB

I

Gleb Alpha's diary:

I went to look at the sandbagged statue
packed in planks.
Custodian and transformer of our ill-starred swamps,
crowned with triumphant victor's laurels,
goggling wide-eyed at the turgid stream,
the bridge and the collegia buildings—yes, yes, named for
    him!—
at the nocturnal shimmer of the Scandinavian Arctic Circle,
at the clouds,
gently highlighted in the late, unfading evening,
but traced out brightly now;
now he resembles a sphinx,
sinking deeper and deeper into corporeal time.
The serpent is hidden:
no doubt it is hissing, pinned under the hoof there inside.
The steed's body is covered by sacks secured with planks,
not even the laurel-crowned horseman's head can be
    discerned.

Atop this Afro-Asiatic construction
towering up from the boulder
—Nikander, I believe, would have smiled—
a few workers in black jackets potter about,
and a hoist is visible—
a beam with a squeaking cable.

They say now it is less obvious from the air,
it does not cast a sharp horse's shadow
with a long tail and a rider,
but some quite obscure shape.
You could say there is no shadow.
In short, the patron of our city,
who gave it his name,
is now following that name
into the realm of phantoms,
where we shall all be soon,
rising up into the rarefied,
golden wartime air.
From there, it is harder and harder to see
the shadow of what is below.
I think, in me, the world has lost
the composer of some new songs—
songs of *Leningrad*.

9 September, 1941
    For the second day, death hails down out of
that pure and golden air.
Yesterday they set the goods station and Badayev warehouses
ablaze
(that must be treason: they clearly aimed their strikes,
guided by signalers firing rockets into the air
right there beside the warehouses).

When the sun set,
they started dropping firebombs. A spine-chilling beauty;
flame-colored glow, sugar flowing along streets,
the smell of burned flour.
And they say that in the zoo,
the elephant and monkeys were snuffed out in an instant.

A hundred-year-old elephant, they say
(which is doubtful):
that means he saw Pushkin.
If so, that was the final link
with the brilliant world,
the shadow of which now lies concealed
beneath the camouflage.

For "the two halves of the universe
yield to the fury of Indra,
and the earth itself quakes at thy frenzy,
oh master of the crushing stones."

15 September

These days a swelter punctuated by raids.
Impossible to sleep—might as well lie down in the park.
Bomb and gas shelters almost useless; dug too shallow.
They don't hit parks yet, though—the Germans have a good
inside man.
Cloudy today. In the western sky,
flashes of fire (our flak cannon in Kronstadt)—
the decisive fighting is there, the fiercest onslaught—
flaring like sheet lightning in the windows of buildings and trams,
flickering on the screen of the air.
Strata of sounds inside my head.
Strange how long the silence lasted,
And then—take that!
Bursting through
in catastrophic counterpoint
before the amazement and horror.

Vera phoned.
    This is madness:
she's still in the city. She says Georgii,
not subject to any call-up,
has donned uniform—the Baltic Fleet—
at his own request
(thank God, not the home militia,
that's certain death in the meat grinder),
that any day now
he heads for the barracks, a translator
monitoring
radio communications.

But I'm a fine one too:
    ashamed to be the cause of everything.

19 September
    The balloons rose up
like viscera ripped open.
Sometimes it seems
the city, convulsed by its injuries,
defends itself by saying to the enemy:
"Come on now, choke
on what you have created—
this bloody slurry."

Cold and windy, gray clouds skimming by.
Impossible to count how many times they've bombed us.
Every two hours precisely: at eight, at ten, at twelve.
The most dreadful raid was at four.
It didn't stop till after midnight.
Along October 25 Prospect,
corpses in puddles,

and above—the crushing gray sky.

Mark, back from the front,
told us
that when a small truck
took a hit in front of them
(there was a film crew in it)
and he saw the shattered bodies,
thighs and feet with white bones poking through the flesh,
he felt aroused.

Death, chow, concupiscence
are fused within us,
it seems to me, into an orgiastic rapture,
which makes the dear, old, euphonic sounds,
linked in my brain with years of work
in the dear old Zubov Art Institute,
pointless.
Here, now, this is Art invading!

I walked, looking at corpses in puddles,
and, like Mark,
ashamed no longer, felt immense arousal.
Sounds moved in two mighty lines,
concluding in assertive exclamations.
A singer and a choir?
Perhaps it is a singer and a choir.
I put Vera on the tram—
Just before the evening raid.
She got home, everything's all right.
Vera! What will happen to Vera?

II

From the diary of Vera Beklemisheva (née Orlik):

The decision is irreversible: to stay. And it's not at all because Gleb has admitted that he will be here until the end, that he won't abandon the papers and the library—this is all a pretext. Who's going to want those papers in a month or two, except maybe for kindling? If the horror isn't over before the winter. So what if there are papers with signatures from Cavos and Verstovsky and even Savromatov (oho!)—several bundles of letters from him to Gleb, he showed them to me: arrogant, admiring, audacious. And it's certainly not because Gleb has admitted that, although he's not subject to the draft, he wishes "to see from close-up the grappling with the pseudo-Aryan wolf, with the darkness that has shrouded the heart of Europe, which . . ."—here you repeated, "it's finished anyway" several times, and something else out of the Rig Veda in a translation by some Müller or other (I haven't read it, God has spared me that). Quite beautiful. He said that the music is awakening in him more intensely than ever, with almost bestial strength, he wants to compose, when he sleeps he hears the harmonies. We walked along Nevsky Prospect—corpses, holes from the bombs, frightened militiamen, one completely bewildered on the corner of Ligovka, looking away like a child—*and in my head*, Gleb tells me, *is the counterpoint of the variations.* But I'm not staying here because of any variations of yours.

In a Moscow prostrate at the feet of Napoleon, Tolstoy's Pierre also wanted *to put an end to the misery of all Europe.* In the final analysis, this is all the private business of Professor G. V. Alpha— what a pretentious seminarian's name that is; and he told me: *it's from Alfani!*—an academic in some institute or other. Put an end to whatever you wish with the power of your understanding, Gleb Vladimirovich. Or with the music that sounds for you, but which all your life you have felt too timid to compose. Well, there's a war on now, it's shameful to feel timid.

Gleb, you should know, the reason I stay here is not at all that I want to share your insanity and the general insanity—war is a joy to your male heart, like all the rest, but for me it is nothing but horror—and not even because I feel infinitely bad about Georgii, who wept when he saw the raw triangle on my back, the scar from our clumsy lovemaking on the floor of your old, tattered apartment, between the piano and the wardrobe, and I babbled something about a hole burned in a blouse, said it was from a candle at a girlfriend's place (what candle, when everyone's had electricity for ages now!)—and before I arrived home, I even burned a blouse with a candle specially. At the back, close to the *os sacrum*. Do you remember that favorite black blouse of mine that I burned a hole in? Gleb, darling, the reason I stay is not shame or love, but this.

Even before everything collapsed and we kissed to the accompaniment of late trolleybuses' electric fireworks at the beginning of summer in the incredibly bright night on Horse Guard Boulevard, lined with its vigilant lime trees, and you told me it was your first time with such a big girl—Gleb, in our Ukrainian family, everyone is broad and strapping, loud, but I'm really the thin one—and you asked me to take off my best shoes with the high heels to level us up (you still haven't got used to it, and you won't, the fact that I'm almost the same height as you), and then you put your head on my shoulder—I remember it all as if it happened only today—and said calmly: "And you'll have my child too."—"Better two."—"All right. A boy and a girl."—that was before we were intimate. Well then: now I'm pregnant. You have the right to think whatever you like, but I know the child is yours. Or the twins. If something happens to me and Georgii reads everything I'm writing, he'll survive. Yes, it sounds cruel, but he'll survive—I know it. And as for you, you won't let anyone see. You'll bury me in yourself. It would be better if you howled.

Gleb, I'm staying because, if you die, I won't be able to keep the child. And why should I? But this way, there's hope.

I'm not going to tell you anything yet.

III

The occupation newspaper *Pravda*, September 1941 (editorial office: 9 Freedom Prospect, Riga):

THE GERMAN ARMY AT
THE GATES OF PETERSBURG

The city is packed with refugees from various regions of Russia
who have been caught in the zone of military operations.
Petersburg is so congested that large numbers of newcomers
spend the night in the open air—in parks, gardens and squares.
The food situation in the city is very grave . . .
Petersburg has the appearance of an armed camp.
Even women and children have been mobilized.
Weapons have been distributed to citizens, even people who
    have never carried one before.
The city is under bombardment by
    long-range guns,
    German heavy artillery,
    brought on railway platforms
    along the Reval-Petersburg line.
The only railway line
    that, until recently, connected Petersburg with the rest of Russia
was the Vologda line, smashed by German air power and littered
with wrecked trains. The rumble of artillery
fire, of German guns aimed exclusively at military
targets, can be heard clearly in the city.
Many inhabitants attempt to escape from Petersburg,

but unsuccessfully. On the outskirts,
a group of children and adults
were captured by German forces
as they tried to break out of the city.
Germans, having fed the refugees,
released both children and adults,
and they returned to Petersburg
and spoke of the warm, open-hearted reception
the Germans gave them,
and their stories contributed
to the rising anti-Soviet mood
of the people of Petersburg . . .

Trapped in the steel-gray ring of German forces,
Soviet Leningrad will fall and, casting off the final fetters
of twenty-four years of communist tyranny,
will be reborn to a bright,
happy and peaceful life
under its glorious historical name—
St. Petersburg!

Workers of the world, unite
for the struggle against bolshevism!

IV

Gleb's diary (continued):

*9–14 October 1941. Days of incessant air raids and the beginning of
the Feast of the Intercession.*
      It is essential for me to write this down, while my mind is
still lucid and my perceptions are clear—at least as the skeleton
of what I can hear, a sketch in words, noting everything that

later, if circumstances permit, will take on acoustic flesh, without allowing the yawning gaps to delay me.

The form is variations—actually double variations: pro and contra, blinding light and deceptive twilight, Alpha and Omega, if you wish (no allusion intended).

Two themes.

A solo kettledrum, with a prelude to a paean of praise. Theme one: on a piano, or even on two pianos, with their lids yawning wide open, displaying the inner strings and ribs of a corporeal soul (for the soul of music is precisely corporeal, although it strives for elemental numericality), its bleeding body. The theme rises in a steady crescendo, in counterpoint with a line of bells. Like a stanza of verse; if you write it down in words, you get this:

City flooded with sunlight	and crowned with flak-cannon explosions
early blanket of snowfall	and a dazzlingly bright spitting rain
river breathing, a stream	through itself ever on-flowing
nevermore can we still	pulsing rhythms in pounding hearts

/ x / x x / x	x / x x / x x / x
/ x / x x / x	x x / x x / x x x
/ x / x x /	x x / x x / x x
x x / x x /	/ x / x / x x /

(The words are only approximate, but I'm sure of the rhythm.)

And the second theme is an *anti*-theme, with the rhythm on a rich cello, in dialogue with a viola, over pale under-painting on a double bass—again I turn it into words

> and gliding like a snake slithering airborne into its strike
> a tree of flame seeking with its roots to drink
> the breath of life of hopes the wafting gust

clearing in an instant the view through the onrushing
atmosphere

(and so:

x / x / x / / x x / x / x x /
  x / x / / x x x / x /
x / x / x / x / x /
  / x x x / x x / x x x / x / x x)

And now the first variation on the first theme, if I continue
filling out the rhythm with words, it sounds approximately like
this:

flooded with bright sunlight   in ragged tattered holes
blossoming through the vapors   roofs and steeple tops
with both the river's lungs   unconstrained by ice
breathing, smoothly whistling   to kettledrum explosions

(this time we'll make do without the schematic—that's all
clear anyway—and quickly rough in the variation on the second
theme):

in the trembling of leaves
    and outline of smoky vines
entwining the breath
    that grows stronger in the final struggle
under the squall of fiery hail
    you are a tree or conflagration

Variation II (first and second themes) is:

as this sunshine of day   glinting so brightly
liquefies the snow   vaporizes drizzle
or sweat on foreheads   with its ardor
you prepare to stand   in the shade of him

 who stands enduringly
  like a revivified blood-bearing tree
 whose bronze hand stretches out above the cold river
 the breath of life, the breath of death in his huge eyes
 that have devoured the thundery atmospheric glint.

Variation III (on the first theme) is:

 infused in life's effulgence
 no, more like a grapevine,
 a shoot of the mortal windstorm
 curved into withies
 you bind the brows of
 the horseman
 towering up mountainlike—

  A dithyramb! It makes an absolutely genuine
 dithyramb!

Chapter Two
VERA

V

"... *Amo, et cupio, et te solum diligo, et sine te jam vivere nequeo: et caetera quis mulieres et alios inducunt, et suas testantur affectionaes.*" For some reason this ironic phrase from Apuleius's *Golden Ass* had stuck firmly in Gleb's mind. It wasn't so much that at certain moments in his life he had felt like Lucius, transformed into an ass (although that had happened), just that the strength of Vera's love, expressed in actions and in words, overflowed the bounds of understanding, making him doubt the reality of what he experienced here, where their happiness intertwined with the general misery.

"This kind of thing doesn't happen," many would have said in his place. "It's undeserved," Gleb told himself. It was as if he had forgotten that what was happening had been earned through years of mistakes and failures, with a host of false moves.

Gleb, like any truly happy man, did not realize what an extreme condition he was in, or how rarely it was experienced in such plenitude. All around there was destruction and war, with the future growing increasingly uncertain. Within, there was the intensity of life and the full scope of its significance. The former seemed like a shadow that had suddenly fallen away, and now, as if recovered from an illness, Gleb walked in a shadowless, sunny space that belonged to neither the autumn nor the city, that was filled with chirping and whistling and flooded with light, encircled by trees that were swayed not by the blasts of bombs and artillery shells but the keen Baltic wind, and the October wind sang with the full-chested breath of the springtime, swirling up the best in him.

"But, when all is said and done, if we are to quote the Romans, then Martial is also right when he asserts that 'wild beasts do not know how to lie,' for now that all the divisions have been removed, we have become precisely wild beasts, left to our own devices, released from the bombed zoo to roam the city at will.

"If only I could have expressed what I was experiencing in music, or, as a last resort, in words. The counterpoint of the music sounding ecstatically within me was a realization that this feeling was doomed to destruction, although now it filled the complete sweep of the horizon and the entire vertical scope of the sky—but my words are too precise and dry, sifting, not in a sunny wind, but in a dry rustle through the fingers seeking to catch them."

To express what he was feeling, Gleb could only choose from the words of others, and the concordance of his inner condition with the mood of all those whose verbal magic he had admired for so long, especially in the days of his youth, only convinced him of the vanity of any attempts to express his feelings in an individual idiom.

Take Arsenii Tatishchev—where was he now, having abandoned our Petrograd, in what distant lands was he wandering? Was he still alive? That almost square little volume, *Lightsound*, published in 1922 on poor paper, with print that rubbed off at the first careless touch, contained acutely sunny lines like this—despite the circumstances in which Tatishchev had composed them:

> Better I should see you thus:
> in angelic essence, in radiance open to the sunlight,
> lowering a foot into water, unclenching into air a hand,
> on which there shall be traced a sign,
> disclosing vision
> through the earth-stems of breathing,
> through the lyre-stringed external.
> Stay somewhere close to me, where elbow can be folded

into elbow, and if there be shadow, it is shadows'
light-scissors,
eyes of radiance, faces of sound . . .

Gleb knew that he could never have written anything like
that.

He remembered very clearly how, at a reading in a Petropolis
that was half-starved—as it was now—given to a crowd muffled
in filthy cast-offs, who listened with rapt admiration, a certain
Iosif Krik and Rodion Narodov, publishers of the bombastic
little journal *Impact*, who more than anything resembled a pair of
back-row grammar-school pupils giving the district inspector a
hard time, had been sadistically stubborn in accusing Tatishchev
of handling verse too formally, of being a bourgeois charlatan,
of allowing an antirevolutionary domination of the free line by
rhyme and meter. Their wretched *Impact* was filled with syrupy,
high-flown, rhetorical "free reflections," from among which Gleb
could remember something about a dead crow being kicked by
an extremely jolly sailor. What could Tatishchev, distinguished by
the fine military bearing of his figure, wrapped in a greatcoat that
gave no warmth against his own inward chill, with his forehead
bisected by a lightning-bolt scar, possibly have conveyed to this
audience?

But Krik and Narodov would have seemed the very model of
integrity in comparison with those who came after them.

All those Young Communists conscripted into literature,
music, and other areas—where had they been swept away by the
somber-black storm of the thirties, which they themselves had
invoked?

Now that a new hurricane had blown in, now that even
those who had previously swept away such fanatical devotees
of radical rhetoric had themselves been swept away, a time of
genuine, not merely verbal, renewal had returned, Gleb tried to

convince himself. And Vera was the personified elemental spirit of the authenticity for which Gleb had yearned so long in the stiflingly Hoffmanesque prewar atmosphere of a city that was half-Petropolis, half-Leningrad.

True, they didn't see each other as often as he would have liked. They were constrained by the life of a city under siege, with mechanically regular artillery bombardments, air raids, and imminent starvation, when simply spending rationing coupons required an intense daily effort. But public transport was still running, there was still electricity, the telephone worked. And the genuinely cold weather was still a long way off.

Gleb also knew that, once in a while, Georgii Beklemishev was allowed home on leave but, strangely, he didn't feel jealous at all.

Vera mentioned once that her period was very late, but Gleb had heard from friends that this had already happened to their wives and girlfriends—owing to the nervous stress of the first weeks of the siege. Every attempt to clarify their feelings only culminated in flinging the two of them together even more intensely. And now, after this intimacy that had swept away all divisions, Gleb once again asked Vera the question that was tormenting him.

He didn't understand that Vera had already made her choice—that she had no right to refuse her husband sympathy and comfort, but that this meant absolutely nothing. On every visit home, Georgii Beklemishev sensed her greater remoteness. For him, the dying of their relationship was muted by his impressions of a life restricted to the barracks, while for Vera it was eclipsed by the irrepressible feeling that engrossed her, body and soul.

An inauthentic life was making way for an authentic, earnest one. But Georgii and Vera Beklemishev were entering that life by different roads.

Had not Gleb himself wanted, twenty years ago, to start over again with a clean slate? Had he not renounced the name of a glorious line of poets and priests—Alfani—one branch of which had even flourished on Baltic shores, in favor of the shrilly post-futuristic and, to certain austere tastes, overly aggressive and uncompromising name of Alpha? Was not he himself a creation of the great rift between the old, which was already past, and the new, which was now advancing implacably? Gleb used these, or similar exalted and rhetorical terms, to explain his own feelings to himself, as if he were seeking a justification for them, as if something still required clarification and justification. In actual fact, he was simply borne along by the current, and did not fully understand its force and direction.

VI

From Gleb's notebook:

Mark came. Knowing my fondness for antiquity, he showed me some photographs taken in September on the roof of the Hermitage on one of the rare cloudless days—while a women's voluntary fire brigade was on duty up there.

Absolutely unpremeditated, like everything in our city, but for all that no less reminiscent of an antique cameo, this conjunction of fire helmets, battered and scratched as a consequence of the bombings and rubble-clearing, but still vibrantly gleaming in the sun, locks of hair curling out from under the helmets, the firewomen's clothing—tight-fitting tarpaulin overalls with wide belts—and their gazes, straining out through the smoky air, over Palace Square and its proud column, over the vases and sculptures round the perimeter of the roof, past the tram creeping toward St. Isaac's, over the horses of the General HQ building, toward the west, with its constant threat of an air raid.

Dressed as if for a Syracusan coin:
    a firewoman in a helmet, ringed with dolphins,
columns and sculptures, planes and sunshine,
    in a drifting crown of flak-cannon bursts.

Vera's profiles are simply superb: I didn't even know she was in that team. "You can keep them—I think you rather like that Beklemisheva girl, don't you?"

I declined, being discreet. This was already more than I should hear in the context of our ostensibly restrained friendship.

He says they probably won't take photographs for the news-paper—they're more by way of photos for the historian, who will "gaze and envy."

But I think this: the sinking-heart moment
    just before the final and most terrible blow—
the sun not yet willing to darken
    in the face of the day-locusts' rustling wings.

VII

According to data from the civil register office, the number of people living in the city of Leningrad and the districts administratively subordinate to it (including Kronstadt) was as follows:

in September 1941	–	2,450,639
in October 1941	–	2,915,169
in November 1941	–	2,485,947

According to centralized data, the number of food-rationing cards issued to the population was:

in September 1941—2,377,600, including 35.1% of the total to workers and Engineering and Technical Personnel, 18.4% to office workers, 28.3% to dependents, 18.2% to children;
in October 1941—2,371,300, including 34.5% to workers and E and T Personnel, 16.7% to office workers, 30.2% to dependents, 18.6% to children;
in November 1941—3,384,400, including 34.5% to workers and E and T Personnel, 15.6% to office workers, 31.1% to dependents, 18.9% to children.

The daily ration allowance of bread was:

from 2 to 12 September 1941—600 grams for workers and E and T Personnel, 400 grams for office workers, 300 grams for dependents, 330 grams for children below the age of 12;
from 13 September to 13 October—400 grams for workers and E and T Personnel, 200 grams for office workers, 200 grams for dependents, 200 grams for children under the age of 12;
from 13 October to 20 November—300 grams for workers and E and T Personnel, 150 grams for office workers, 150 grams for dependents, 150 grams for children under the age of 12;
from 20 November to 25 December—250 grams for workers and E and T Personnel, 125 grams for office workers, 125 grams for dependents, 125 grams for children under the age of 12.

VIII

Fyodor Chetvertinsky to Julius Pokorny:

Esteemed colleague,

A strange business, when even the post to Vasilievsky Island and the Petrograd Side takes an eternity to arrive, that I should get the idea of writing to you. War and Fire (our Russian *ogon*—that same mighty Agni who holds sway in the nether regions of the earth) do not separate us, but unite us, who are on opposite sides of the blazing storm. And since you and I, dear colleague, are not Kshatriyas, but sages, our work, our spell possesses, so to speak, a supreme, all-embracing power. Exceptional circumstances set aside all superfluities. Therefore, permit me, in writing from here, in this city firmly secured with a lock of iron, to Belgium, with its lace-and-lilies decorations, to address you not as "Herr Doktor Professor," but "Julius." I hope this familiarity will not anger you.

You must agree that the invention of the wheel—which, according to your classification, is victoriously proclaimed by the proto-root *k^wék^{w}lo-/*k^wol-o-—has not been of any great benefit to the Indo-Europeans.

On this same wheel
several of the tribes that have deviated from the general
    meaning,
having trundled and rattled across Belgium with their
    motorized divisions,
have reached the outskirts of the most wonderful of all cities
created by Russians, the name of which the Romanovs,
at a time predating the skirmish
with our present adversaries
were quick, with their Germanophile understanding,
to translate as "Petrograd."
I categorically object: you were born in Prague,

there is no need to explain to you that burg(h) derives, not
    from a word for "city,"
but from a fortified, exalted, radiant—*bheregh-,
bherghos-—place.
And we shall be that Rocky Shore
on which they will shatter.
To the west is the ocean, and we are an embankment, land.
After all, we are not Russian *lokhi*, spotted salmon,
—a fish of the common Indo-European proto-homeland—
splashing in their rivers,
or beeches (*buk* in Russian—could that be where it's from?)
rustling around their Prussian Königsberg,
They will yet be humbled
by our stout oaks.

    But if you and I are right, the third thing,
after the salmon and the beech,
that language preserves from the maternal landscape is
the Proto-Indo-European *sneiguh-,
which, to some, is memory,
but to us—as snow, our *sneg*—a shield and comrade,
who will be our trusty armor.
And, arrayed in this snow's freezing cold,
armed with the power of thunderbolts,
seated, like our steppeland forebears,
on fleet steeds (*ekuo-s)
we shall fuck
(*iebh-—now there is a most ancient root,
and clearer than ever to us now!)
our foes
until we ram them back
up into the maternal vulva,
into the womb of their fear (*pīzdā-, as you write it).

Yes, yes. All the way up the cunt.
So there! Such shall be the fate
of all degenerates.
And our foe still dares speak
of your and our 'inferiority'!

I should also like to observe that, having found ourselves
in the Finno-Ugrian marshes,
in the swamps of a neighboring world, amid its overflowing
    rivers,
not only have we stood firm,
but with a "wave of the hand" from our leader, immortalized
    as a bronze idol,
whose equestrian monument—
which is only seemly for tribesmen of the Eurasian plain—
we have ritually covered with earth (dry, sandy)
and even shielded with planks,
and round him raised up the stone citadel of "Piterburkh,"
with a royal burial-mound (now!) at its center,
but also, despite the siege, we still gaze proudly round
at the boundless, flat, amicable east,
at the free and open north,
and at the south, from whence we came,
and, of course, at the presently hostile west and northwest.
It is precisely now that we, our language, our power, our
    memory must hold out
—the fate of a continent
and the fundamentals common
to the Indo-Europeans of its expanses is being decided.
We shall assuredly endure,
because we are closer to the roots,
we are freer, we are more wholesome.
We simply cannot perish.

Our neighbors, the Finns
are already playing it safe—taking the city by storm is not for
   them.
But even the Germans, when they are pounded
by the thousand thousand hooves
of the Russian avalanches that they have called down on
   themselves,
after all the storms that will sweep over them,
will be needed—yes, yes, they will be needed!
—and not as enemies trampled into the dust,
but—and do not be surprised, Julius—
as allies.
Only first let them string up on the trees they revere
—beeches?—very well, let it be beeches!—
which grow in Eastern, kindred, Baltic Prussia—
all their buffoons.
Let them scrape off themselves
all that poisonous stuff, all the cultural corruption,
and stand shoulder-to-shoulder
in the common cause of establishing
a common *Lebensraum*.
But that will be later, Julius,
much later. First—the disgrace of defeat.

   For after all, a language is predictive, it is all there.
including our inevitable
victory.

I remain yours etc.,
   Fyodor Svyatopolk-Chetvertinsky

Not having previously been inclined to versification, and being
given to a rather ponderous and stubborn mode of thought,

Fyodor Stanislavovich felt pleased: the letter had turned out nothing at all like an article on linguistics and sounded like a perfectly genuine poem.

IX

Georgii Beklemishev to Yulia Antonovna Beklemiksheva in Saratov (checked by the military censor):

Dear Mama!

Good to hear that you have settled in at the new place: things will be quieter for you there.

Everything's secure here. We battle on with a firm belief in speedy victory over the Hitlerite invaders. Thanks to the wise concern shown by the command and the city authorities, firm norms have been established for food allowances. When leave is permitted, I go home on a tram. The cold weather has come early, and it has been snowing since 12 October! The power is still on and our glorious Leningrad water supply is working. It has been suggested that, on an individual basis, people should lay in a supply of plywood to replace broken windows (so far not a single one in our rooms has been damaged by shrapnel or bomb blasts) and also fuel for heating during what is clearly going to be a very cold winter.

After managing to sell Uncle Kolya's series of engravings of the El Djem amphitheater and the Roman ruins at Dougga, I bought a welded metal stove at the market, especially for the winter cold. I feel bad about the prints, but now the sun of North Africa will warm Vera and our entire Beklemishev lair in an entirely material sense. I am in a profoundly combative mood.

The only strain is with Vera: we are drifting apart. She is no longer as quick-tempered as she was before you left in August, and outwardly everything is fine: we get on together amicably,

Vera is benignly affectionate and even, in a blank sort of way, resigned to our new circumstances. But only outwardly. You were right when you told me that not every beautiful arrangement can genuinely enhance and adorn a life, and Vera, it seems to me now, was precisely such an arrangement, a graft onto the Beklemishev way of life that has failed to take. What is in her heart is a mystery to me. I love her, of course, very much, but I think it is safer for Vera and better for my peace of mind if she joins you, and then— after our speedy victory—we shall see.

My rather poor—I realize that now—painting, all those imitations of the cubists or the fauves, stripy orange hippopotami on the Bank Bridge, bathed in blue light and besieged by dogs with wings of fire, now seem absolutely ludicrous in comparison with the immense, unifying cause propelling us all forward, and so following the imminent conclusion—I truly believe it is imminent—of this war, I am hardly likely to take up the brush again.

Dear Mama, I hope always to hear that you are in good health. Don't worry too much about me, and I shall feel better for the knowledge of your encompassing warmth and affection.

I kiss you.

Your loving son,

Second lieutenant

Georgii Beklemishev

X

Gleb knew Yulia Beklemisheva slightly from the second half of the 1910s. Recalling this made Gleb realize that he was no longer young himself.

The wife of a well-known financier, she hailed from one of the Volga provinces: her father was a middling sort of land owner there and Beklemisheva regarded her husband Vasilii Mikhailovich's business affairs and acquaintances with a certain disdain, as if she didn't notice that they provided her with an extremely luxurious life, and even in speaking of Beklemishev's most important business partner, the venerable Afanasii Svyatogorsky (his rather odd grandson, also Afanasii, was known to Gleb as the composer of the esoterically cacophonous or, as Afanasii junior called it, "ultrachromatic" music to his *Concluding Spectacle*, which he had written in imitation of Scriabin)—when speaking of grandfather Svyatogorsky behind his back, she always called even him a "crook" and a "shyster" (it was probably well deserved). However, she could discuss with relish and at great length the details of the Beklemishevs' genealogy and the consanguinity of her husband's ancestors with illustrious princely families.

In her eyes, possessing a title and pedigree was enough to brand anyone as "cultured." This could not be explained away as the result of her provincial-backwater upbringing. It was a fundamental trait of her general outlook.

She often alluded with pride to her growing son Georges, the "new Beklemishev," emphasizing that the heir had a considerable talent for languages and drawing, and in that, as far as his character was concerned, he mostly took after her. As usual in such cases, Yulia Antonovna passed over in silence the fact that he had inherited some of his traits from the Beklemishev side—the financier's brother, Nikolai Mikhailovich, was a rather good engraver and had traveled widely and frequently in the Mediterranean.

When the Provisional Government came to power, Vasilii Mikhailovich, realizing that the end of his life of luxury was near at hand, decided to have one last fling. Without informing his wife, in the summer of 1917 he purchased a magnificent mansion in Moscow, designed by Schechtel and artistically furnished with his brother Nikolai's assistance, and moved into it with his long-standing girlfriend, a singer from the Yar restaurant, whom he had previously only visited occasionally. Yulia Antonovna reacted to her husband's decampment in predictable fashion: how could anyone exchange Petersburg for mercantile Moscow and a wife of noble blood (Yulia Antonovna's own genealogy remained a mystery to Gleb) for a rootless gypsy girl?

It was strange, but this melodramatic affair, as well other stories about the Beklemishev family, had lodged firmly in Gleb's memory—most likely because that was the time when he and the Svyatopolk-Chetvertinskys became close.

It was in their spacious and hospitable home that Gleb first saw Yulia. Despite the revolutionary times, the Svyatopolk-Chetvertinskys carried on living in the same grand style as before: they had an automobile and servants, and they did not begrudge themselves the expenditure of substantial sums of money on gourmandizing and other extravagances of various kinds, such as supporting an entire publishing house, at which the manager, editor, and—frequently—proofreader was Sergei Stanislavovich Chetvertinsky, who was five years older than Gleb and had dropped the aristocratic "Svyatopolk" from their double-barreled name, together with the aristocratic title of "prince," when he was still a student. Sergei's brother, Fyodor, was a linguist and a bit of a philosopher. They both thought about things in more or less the same way. They saw what was happening as a clarification of the foundations of Russian reality, the return of the current to its proper, direct course.

The Chetvertinskys combined Little Russian gourmandizing with a certain un-aristocratic and very definitely un-Petersburgian sociability. Gleb, who visited their home at first on publishing business (Sergei had invited him to manage the scholarly section of his enterprise), soon began to feel a distinct need for the kind of company—so intelligent, lively, and free, distinguished by its breadth of political and cultural outlook, comfortable but by no means lordly—that no other house could provide for him.

Beklemishev's grass widow, who also became a frequent visitor, had quite definite designs on Sergei.

Eventually Sergei confessed to Gleb that, for all of Yulia's superficial attractiveness, and her sculptural proportions (these features were later passed on to her son), she palpably "lacked fire," and not even her genealogical folly could compensate for the inner "brittleness" of a twenty-seven-year-old woman exhausted by her solitary state.

No serious relationship developed and Yulia Beklemisheva eventually disappeared (to surface later in the role of Vera's mother-in-law). The fate of her runaway husband remained unclear. The former financier was apparently arrested by the Bolsheviks, and then released to set the banking system in order, after which he asked to be allowed to leave the country—at that point Vasilii Mikhailovich's tracks had been lost to sight. His scandalous departure from the family probably saved the Beklemishevs from persecution. Perhaps other circumstances, unknown to Gleb, also intervened—the kind it was not done to speak of aloud.

But Gleb was not in the least surprised when he heard from Vera that after war was declared, Yulia Antonovna started turning the subject of conversation to how, at last, "Europeans will come and put things in order in Ingermanland, and now everything will be the way it used to be." And he was even less surprised when, before the bombing had begun and the long-awaited "coming of the Europeans" had taken place, mother Beklemisheva made haste to evacuate the area, or simply ran away, while things were being "put in order," to her relatives in the Volga region. The "coming of the Europeans" could take its course, but nothing must threaten Yulia Beklemisheva's personal safety.

XI

The city really was reverting to the wild, regressing to its primordial swampy state. Whether this was good or bad was hard to say. Fyodor Chetvertinsky, who remembered very clearly the first reversion to the wild that had occurred between 1919 and 1922, saw something cyclical in this, a reminder to the inhabitants of "Petrograd (vulgo Finnopolis)," as a certain nineteenth-century wit used to call the city, of the kind of ground on which it was constructed—after the manner of seismic shocks in tectonically unstable regions.

By virtue of his cast of mind, Fyodor Chetvertinsky himself was interested in linguistic ground (it's all in the language!), the percolation of Indo-European meanings into the Finno-Ugrian substratum that was taking place even before the Russians, inspired by the vision of Peter I, decided to build their most important city here. Chetvertinsky's intention was to fathom the objective laws of those semantic references to nature that had shaken the foundations of the beautifully constructed ensemble, the rhythm, as he called it in his own thoughts, of reminders "of what was here before."

And what was here before?

A point of intersection between Finno-Ugrian and Baltic, Slavic and Germanic, a place where words and meanings were exchanged, and also, later, rites and goods, customs and faith.

Here the Hanseatic League, which included our Novgorod, became the Russian "crowd" and "folk," which is to say *kansa*: trading gold was called *kulta*, sweet honey (the Russian *myod*—which refers to mead as well as the gift of the bees) had the affectionate name of *mesi*, and the name for the ruling prince—the *kuning* or "konung"—was *kuningas*. The family (Russian *semya*) or *seim*—the general council of the Balts—became *heimo*; our Russian word for "apple," *yabloko*, shifted northward, sounded like *apila*, and signified "clover." But the rye (*rozh* in Russian) or *ruis*, set seed as it ripened, and the leaves (Russian *listy*) of both trees and books—*lehti*—rustled in the wind, and any huge Finno-Ugrian *ogor* ("eel"—in Russian *ugor*), or *ankerias* in the local tongue, slithered through the waters of the long lake or *järvi* (Russian *yar*—"ravine"); or—if they were sea eels—through the shallow waters of the Baltic, to Yura, the slightly salty (*suola!*) *meri* (in Russian *morie*—"sea"). These were words understood by both sides, a common stratum in the foundations of the city, a solid layer in the boggy delta.

But in that case, Fyodor Stanislavovich said to himself, we should have eaten Finnish victuals. But which ones? Lingonberry jelly. Oh, blissful delicacy for the ravenously hungry! Lokh-salmon in its own sauce, *graavi lohi*, or—in the dialect more comprehensible to the Finn—*lohi omassa liemessään?* The recipe is simple: take the sliced fish and add salt, sugar, pepper, dill, and brandy (if there isn't any, then Armenian cognac); marinate in this mixture for twelve hours.

"And there's also a rather good salad, one of those that our cook used to prepare—*rassol*," Chetvertinsky heard someone reply, and discovered that he was standing at the exit from the Public Library in Cathy's Garden, beside a short, poorly shaved individual in a threadbare, dirty coat with a bundle of books under his arm. "You boil potatoes, carrots, and beetroot, add a pickled cucumber and an onion, chop everything finely and dress it with cream, vinegar, and sugar-beet syrup . . ."

"What's Finnish about that? It's simply our Russian *vinegret*."

"The Finnish part is the herring."

"Yes, interesting. Bye-bye!"—and Chetvertinsky set off across October 25 Prospect toward the boarded-up Yeliseev Grocery Store. Trying to suppress thoughts of food, in which even a simple little salad appeared as a magical, fairy-tale dish—potatoes! carrots! beetroot! onions! ravishing fish!—he started drawing together his fragmentary thoughts about the particular and the

general, about the tectonic jousting of intellectual plates, collid-
ing with each other in ways that set his head spinning and the
ground sliding out from under his feet.

The family crest of the Chetvertinskys—of the Orthodox,
primordial branch, which had never intermarried with
the bloodthirsty Viking Riurikoviches or the Germanized
Romanovs—was St. George on horseback, impaling the dragon
writhing under his mount's hooves. As a linguist, as a man given
to generalizations, Fyodor Stanislavovich realized what stood
behind this profound image preserved for centuries:

Lightning discharges of atmospheric
forces granting breath, dilating soul and spirit,
wreaking havoc with those other forces,
who get under the hooves of the fearless nomads,
kings of the fecund continent, mounted Kshatriyas,
those eternally subverting and invading,
poisoning consciousness with the accursed bane of "cultured"
  resignation,
banishing us from the Eden of potent, vigorous life
(which is immortality, for it knows no end, and fears it not).
Doubt, inaction, and negation,
opposing honor, faith, action, fidelity.

And although Fyodor Stanislavovich's own path was
somewhat different—understanding, and through understanding,
the conservation of wisdom and its millennial truths—he felt
infinite respect for the Kshatriya-warrior, guarding the peace
of the earth, and the noble-ploughman, sowing this earth with
seeds and meanings. For him, everything that was happening,
especially the war, was a stripping-bare of the eternal triad of
wisdom-fearlessness-labor—the scouring away, like hard scum, of
all else. We have no need for boundless doubting and questioning

of the nature of things, if this nature is given to us in direct, lived experience and action. Let it be laid bare even further, down to the very foundations, through what is happening to us. Does not the temptation of the serpent lie in questioning what is already clear? Is this not the sin of Adam and Eve? We have taken it as the beginning of our history, we accept it—but even our history must come to an end sometime.

Let everything that is happening, Chetvertinsky continued thinking, lead to the release—with a thrust of a metaphorical spear—of the sun of light, the sun of truth. And the ruin, the destruction of my body, your body, our common body will not be terrible, for it will lay the foundation of a new world.

A sudden suspicion occurred to him: then is not the sacrifice of all who are now imprisoned in the besieged city, our destruction, precisely a ritual sacrifice, and therefore inescapable in the laying of a new foundation? And what is there to fear in this—after all, we're all going to die anyway. "And I myself, completing and expressing the thoughts of my brother Sergei, and in a sense living out his life in our city—am not I, metaphorically at least, his murderer? Romulus sacrificing Remus in the name of the Fourth, eternal, and everlasting Rome?" As yet, Chetvertinsky didn't have an answer to this final question.

XII

The back of beyond, on Vasilievsky Island, where Vera lived, was of no interest to anyone but local residents even before the war, and since the air raids began, the Germans had taken no interest in it either, unwilling to make the effort to shell this sector on any kind of regular basis. Since public transport to the area was operating regularly and efficiently—the immense Leonov Tram Depot was close by—Vera's "isolation" there could be regarded as a blessing.

At least, Gleb tried to persuade himself that this was so. Accustomed to solitude, after so many years, he even accepted the frequent separations from his beloved—which would have been unthinkable if Vera lived in the central area of the city— as inevitable. There was nothing left for Vera to do but console herself with the thought that she only needed to step onto the running board of the number 4 tram and, if all went well (i.e., if no air raid or artillery bombardment siren was sounded), in about twenty minutes she would be near Uritsky Square, at the very beginning of October 25 Prospect, where she could easily change to the number 24 or 34, and there in front of her would be the door of the dear, precious apartment on Labor Square, her genuine, not merely formal home, where her entire being reverberated to her happy heartbeat.

To imagine herself setting off for there, not in a jangling fish tank—clattering past the extinguished torch beacons at the Stock Exchange, across the Bridge of the Republic, with its always dazzling panorama of Peter the Great's collegia buildings and the Admiralty, all greatly improved in appearance over this autumn, then passing the Hermitage, where Vera still worked—to imagine herself traveling there not in a tram but instead clattering her heels over the fine early snow for an hour and a half, along the lines, as the island's streets were called, from west to east, turning to take a shortcut along Vera Slutskaya Street onto Proletarian Victory Prospect, and from there a right turn toward Lieutenant Schmidt Bridge—no, despite all the changes, this was something she could not yet do.

XIII

From Gleb's notebook:

12 November 1941

The music of the blockade:
Tchaikovsky on the radio,
during the shelling and bombing—
a metronome (heartbeat), and then a fanfare (the all clear).

Today at the piano from early morning—
it's Sunday, after all,
not a working day for many at the Zubov Institute—
to the ten-minute knocking of the metronome
        (and exploding shells)—
I played the score of Askold Radziwiłł's "Hymn to Perun."
The "Hymn" once made a strong impression on me.
And Askold himself—skinny and nervous—
Astounded me with a titanic power,
which seemed to exist apart from his
physical being
and the absurd name
given to him
by his music-loving father,
in honor of his favorite opera—
fancy calling your son after Verstovsky's *Grave*!
No, the composer of the "Hymn" resembled least of all,
that rowdy soldier,
killed in a feud by a Varangian prince,
but there was a palpable whiff
of Faustian harmonies,
something only part-Slavonic.
No surprise, then, that another Radziwiłł,
whose score for *Faust*
was approved by Goethe,
was a relative of his.

I remember too how Savromatov—

high-spirited, white-toothed,
savagely audacious—
and I dismantled this "Hymn"
into its component parts,
then screwed it back together
into the motley-colored "Sunthunder."

Now that a genuine abyss
has gaped open within and without,
it's not "Sunthunder,"
or the tectonic shift
of "Hymn to Perun" that moves me,
but a force
that exorcises the avalanche,
that draws the elements into itself
and transforms them
alchemically
into the gold of keen-edged feeling—
say, Tchaikovsky's *Manfred*
sounding continuously from the speaker.

And where is N. N. Savromatov now?
Under a brilliant, sunny sky
in Tbilisi? Alma-Ata?
Composing martial music
far away from the war?
There has been no news from Nikander for a long time.

And Radziwiłł—is he in Paris?
    In New York? In Rio de Janeiro?
When leaving, he played me in farewell
his newly composed pieces—
laconic in the Japanese style—

"Utterances" for an ensemble of soloists
(voice, three instruments—the set of instruments can vary).
It was the same "Hymn to Perun,"
compressed and desiccated, penned into little cells of sound.
Let us reply to that farewell performance,
not in notes, but in words
about our great and famous deeds,
also in the Japanese manner:

Snow falls, trolleybuses creep along
They have taken Klodt's horses
down off the Anichkov Bridge.
A shell has smashed the railings
with the seahorses and nereids.
Enemy at the gates!

Strange,
          before, I used to think I was an art historian,
but here I sit now, writing something like verse, a kind of music.
Mark believed
he was a writer,
he had a quite decent book at the printer
about Savromatov (I helped him with his research),
and now he turns out to be a colossal talent
in photography—incisive vision, the ability
to halt the moment as it becomes myth!
Khlebnikov of the visual image.

What is astounding is not this,
but the supreme excitation

of consciousness strained to the limit
in the vice grip of catastrophe.

15 November

I also ran into Mordovtsev (a relative of the novelist). He was walking along Garden Street with an aimless, smoldering look in his eyes, beard in disarray, and a substantially sunken stomach. Where to?—That's obvious. It was a quiet day: there was almost no shelling. Mordovtsev was carrying a little lapdog, trembling with fright. "How are you getting on, Alexei Petrovich?" He started as he walked along and then, recognizing me, gave a slightly guilty smile: apparently in anticipation of a satisfying supper. Just to be on the safe side he stuffed the little dog inside his coat and kept pushing its head back in all the time as we talked.

"Getting by as best we can, Gleb Vladimirovich."—"And how's your research on Finno-Ugrian antiquity?" During the Finnish campaign Mordovtsev had discovered quite a lot of Moksha in himself and developed a keen interest in animism, and was hoping to make use of it after the Red Army's successful advance on Helsingfors, where Mordovtsev believed that the post of Head of Folklore was awaiting him at the central university of the future Finnish republic of the USSR. At that same time, the winter of 1939–1940, he gave a paper at the Art Institute

about two Finno-Ugrian
heroes in the Russian epics—

Ilya Muromets, both lethargic and idle,
and reinforced in this by the Orthodox religion
(this was a pointed jibe),
and his fortunate rival Tövkse the pagan,
who settled among seven oaks
regarded as sacred by the Slavs,
taking possession of them
and thereby blocking Ilya the contemplative's
route from the forested, Moksha, Oka-Don region

across the steppe to troubled Kiev,
while knocking the lummox-hero out of his saddle with a
    mere whistle—
he was known to his Russian neighbors by the name
of Nightingale the Robber.
From the same lecture I learned that the Absheron Regiment
    soldier, Platon Karataev,
calm, suffering without grief, warmhearted, unhasting,
is an incarnation of the Moksha world outlook
(the tartarized Karatais are related to the Mokshas),
that there were numerous Mokshas in Attila's army
during the sacking of Rome,
that subsequently there was an alliance between Mokshas
    and Volga Sarmatians,
and that the name of the Erzyans, close to the Mokshas,
goes back
to the Sarmatian *arsan*, meaning "courage."
It turned out that the Russians' rivals in the struggle for the
    legacy
of the departing lords of the Eurasian plain—the
    Sarmatians—
were Finno-Ugrians who whistled like nightingales
in the wild Ryazan (Erzyan),
Muromian,
Meshcheran,
Upper Volga forests,
which even Genghis Khan's forces feared to enter,
and their wild, lawless whistle,
which somehow did not tally well with Alexei Petrovich—
reserved in manner, although giving free rein to his fantasies,
red-cheeked, life-loving, and law-abiding,
certainly more Karataev's heir than the Nightingale's—
this whistling was heard

even in the remote corners of the continent.

It had to be admitted that all this contained a fair dose of typically ingenious intelligentsia wit, but it struck a deep chord even in me. "You're joking, of course!" my chance-met acquaintance said, frowning. "Oh, no indeed. Look how much invaluable material there is in everyday reality: little by little we are returning to the pre-Petrine paradise, to 'the refuge of the wretched Finn.'"— "You know, I don't have any time now. I hope we shall succeed in crushing the loathsome Finno-Germanic reptile that has reduced us ..."—a gesture in the direction of the trembling dog's head that had stuck itself out of his coat again—"... to such unheard-of, one might say, *abomination*. Farewell!" I was clearly distracting him from something he had been looking forward to for a long time. I refrained from raising the question of whether it was worthy for the descendants of the wild Nightingale Odikhmantievich to sink to the level of hunting domestic pets. "As you wish, Alexei Petrovich, I hope we shall see each other again."—"We are all in God's hands" (the recent former pagan crossed himself).

I am very hungry. Always, under any circumstances. Even making entries in this notebook doesn't distract me from thoughts that are clearly obsessive.

I'm starving!

PART TWO:
WINTER

Chapter Three
"PITINBRUKH NIGHTS"

XIV

Capital uproarious,
Pitinbrukh the glorious:
feast on anything you want
in cellars and in restaurants.

In December's breezy chill
I got loaded to the gills,
talked to myself and couldn't stop,
outside Yeliseev's shop.

XV

A jotting by F. S. Chetvertinsky:

5 December 1941

This is the menu nowadays:

1. If you boil a ten-centimeter-square piece of the skin of some animal (a cow is good, but sometimes it's a cat, a dog, or even a rat: by the way, cat meat is like rabbit), and soak a ten-centimeter-square sheet of carpenter's glue in it, with a certain degree of skill it produces a fine, nourishing broth-jelly. We've eaten it and enjoyed it.

2. There was this delicacy: sliced earth from the Badaev Warehouses. Evdokiya Alexeevna and I bought a substantial amount. It lasted until December. The taste is like fatty cottage cheese, saturated in oil and melted

sugar. We poured boiling water over it. It is all just a memory now. But it's no sin to relish this too (in the mind's eye).

The most important things: to take care of yourself, to wash, and—for me—to shave; to stay out of your bed as long as possible, to wash one's clothes and sheets, to keep moving, to save food (crumbs).

People die seemingly from sheer exhaustion, without complaining of anything, from low blood pressure, from wear and tear on the heart and internal organs: when he's starving, a man burns up his body, like the kerosene in a primitive lamp. So if you walk along the street, the best advice for the weak is: walk against the wind, leaning into it, and try not to fall on your back. Fall on your back, and it's almost certainly the end.

But hunger is a taboo topic. Like alcohol for a chronic drunkard.

Although it generates an intense inner excitation.

XVI

From Gleb's notebook:

Mark has delighted me with his photographs again.
He showed me "the city's ears,"
installed on the Peter and Paul Fortress.
Bundles of four sound-locator trumpets,
familiar to everyone from posters,
aimed up at the sky,
each with a metal chair attached;
and a unit of four soldiers
on duty in earphones day and night,
calculating distances
to invisible singing objects,

so that any plane,
even above the clouds—
and sunshine is rare now—
risks running into a barrage of flak.

The bundles of bell-mouthed pipes
reminded me
of the three trumpets on the Radziwiłł crest,
ringed round with: *Bóg nam radzi* (God Advises Us).
Proud Askold Radziwiłł showed me them before he left,
when I was gathering material about his distant relative,
Antoni, Duke of Posen—
the same man who composed
music for Goethe's *Faust*.

Where is it now,
the Radziwiłł family's Europeanness?

Those who have read *Faust*
(properly, one must admit),
now dominant—or so they think—in the air,
are striving to bomb us all
into the gelid expanse of the ice-bound delta.

Well then, what does God "advise" us?
What does He "say" to us?
That with such a highly acute
musical ear, no amount of wild
cavorting by those unhinged demons
can make us afraid?
That no winter of crushing hunger
will ever smear us into snowy Nothingness?

My heart listens to space singing,
but its response is only sullen silence.

XVII

From Vera Orlik's diary:

14 December 1941
Two days now since the trams stopped running.
At least 20⁰ Celsius below.
I barely made it to the Hermitage.
This afternoon, at four, more shelling.
I didn't go back:
for the first time I stayed at Gleb's place to warm up
(he doesn't mind). Even if Georgii
shows up at home out of the blue,
it doesn't matter now. I'm writing
on a narrow strip and afterward
I'll have to glue it in
(the letters barely fit onto the line)
to highlight this red-letter day:
the final and complete abandonment
of the prewar "proprieties."
The water mains still work here,
but there's no electricity.
An open kerosene lamp hangs over the piano.
I managed to take a bath—how wonderful!
We heated water on the stove, burning bound files
of thick musical journals.
Gleb laughed: "The cheap hacks smoke too much.
If need be, we'll use *Goethes sämtliche Werke*
for our kindling."

There was no strength left for love—
we simply kept each other warm.

15 December (on the back of the strip)
    Gleb brewed up a small handful of coffee
(he bought it in August
at Yeliseev's shop, was saving it
for just such an "extraordinary
occasion"). That was a real celebration!
Afterward he walked me to work,
and in the evening to Vasilievsky.
He says a brisk stroll through the freezing snow
to sounds of gunfire from the front
is good for him
(in his emaciated state!).
Nearing Smolensky Cemetery,
an endless succession
of funeral processions
across Mussorgsky Prospect, beside the tram depot:
some with little sleds, a few with carts.
And in homemade cardboard coffins,
or simply swathed in rags
or dirty sheets—the larva-bodies.
People bringing their dear ones,
like some ancient Egyptian ritual.
Gleb said, "As if now they'll load them
onto barks sailing to the setting of the sun."
The sun, incidentally, was hidden.
Nothing but the rumble of guns, the blizzard, bright flashes
all the way along the horizon.

XVIII

On the way back from Vasilievsky Island, under fierce artillery fire, Gleb kept recalling several lines by Arsenii Tatishchev, from the middle of *Lightsound*, and marveling at the power of Tatishchev's forward-looking vision: after all, the verse that had suddenly resurfaced was probably written in October 1919, when winter had not really started yet and the guns were only whooping somewhere over near Gatchina, although the sound could still be heard in the central districts of the city. But as Tatishchev's imagination heard things, it was "winter" that rhymed with the deadly shelling, and that was the only way he could capture in words that cruel autumn, with the specters of inevitable winter hunger and restoration haunting the city.

> ... blazing up in flame and boiling
> out through the blossoming arches,
> clamped under-hoof, but still roiling—
> what a rhyme!—it sears and scorches,
>
> snowing down on us in soot,
> in a winter of big guns roaring,
> this air; and we can neither look
> away nor hear Wells's "Ulla!" ringing
>
> through the rumble and the clamor,
> it's men, not Martians, who are flinging
> earth over our eyes in a dark shower,
> in a winter of big guns flashing ...

It wasn't Martians now, either, and definitely not people, but some third thing. And although Gleb tried, he couldn't formulate it, he couldn't find the right word for the nonhuman, mechanical principle at work. His mind worked away doggedly at the problem, though there was probably no point in solving it anyway.

XIX

From Gleb's notebook:

16 December 1941 and after
     The hunger is so bad,
     that even the fever
     of the agitated brain
     recedes—

continuing from November
in modo giapponese,
here are the final spasms:

Trolleybuses halted
on white-frosted Horse Guard Prospect.
Windows smashed out.

*

People dragging things on sleds.
Trucks frozen into streets
flooded by burst pipes
here and there.

*

Motionless trams.
Broken streetlamps.
Snapped-off power lines.

*

But someone still walks cheerfully into the snowstorm
with his briefcase and fur coat.
This someone is still smiling.
People still carry bundles by.
Men still feel hot (unbuttoned).
They still expect evacuation—
on the train to the lake
(to the sounds of shelling).

*

A burst water main:
water gushing unceasingly
from the hydrant by St. Isaac's.
They scoop up the unfrozen water
from holes in the ice
in the middle of the street,
some with mugs, some with ladles.

*

Toward midwinter—the climax
of the nightmare. At the flea market
they trade:
matches, soap, shag tobacco,
oilseed pulp and excess clothes
for crude chunks of bread.

*

It has gotten warmer: on the sleds

they take stitched-up bodies to the morgue,
where they load them into trucks—
and dump them into the mass graves.

*

The guns of Baltic Fleet ships,
frozen in the Neva, fire into the air.
Paying no attention to the firing,
people shuffle along the Neva,
going here or there.
December in Petropolis.

XX

From Vera's diary (on narrow strips of paper):

22 December 1941.
        The shortest day of all.
The snow has thawed, turned black.

Today, under the guise of an inspection,
Mark Nepshchevansky,
Gleb's oldest friend—
Gleb no longer feels shy around anyone—
took us to view the storerooms
at the Museum of Atheism and Religion.
So this is what they've been hiding from us:
the original—or a copy?—
of the miraculous Virgin of Kazan
(and they said it was lost),
the remains of St. Seraphim,
wrapped up in cellophane,

and hundreds of other
wonder-working relics and icons:
Soviet catacombs
in the primordial style,
at the very center of a modern city,
with noisy tram and trolley lines—
silent now—close by,
right under the archway of Kazan Cathedral,
which the enemy is shelling,
kept under seven seals of mystery,
with the natural temperature
of profound, eternal sleep.

The church would never
have thought of this.

Mark is a terribly successful fellow
at the central TASS photo corps:
welcome everywhere, knows everyone.
He stood aside, not interfering,
with his brand new Kodak,
and smiled. Smiles are rare now.

A city of shadows—everywhere
we wear our fluorescent badges.
Especially here, in the gloomy
labyrinths of hope and faith.

God, Gleb has got so gaunt.
Peering with a bright, feverish glint—
immense eyes, in constant motion—
from under hair that has matted
beneath his ludicrous cap

(he says it keeps him warm).
And he talks of nothing but food and music!

But at the sight of all these treasures,
set out along the shelves,
no longer afraid of being noticed—
if need be, I'll just say: "I see better like this"—
I kneel down silently and pray.
Mark—an atheist, as befits
a successful bon vivant—
stood to one side.
But Gleb whispered something
with his eyes closed:
ah, what a pity
that now he is ashamed
of the feelings surging through him.

XXI

St. Mitrophan of Voronezh to Pyotr Romanov, in the Year of our
Lord 1682:

You will raise up a great city
in honor of the holy apostle Peter.
It will be a new capital.
God blesses you to do this.
The Icon of Kazan will be a protecting veil
to the city and all your people.
For as long as the icon remains in the capital
and Orthodox Christians pray before it,
no enemy shall set foot in the city.

XXII

Tsar Peter saw
that the holy icon of the Mother of God
did through God's grace work many wonders,
and took it as the guide
for his army and on the day of battle with the Swedes
made it his shield and protection,
and did vanquish his enemy utterly with the aid of the Mother
 of God,
and did place this perfect stone,
Thy miraculous icon,
in the foundation of a new ruling city,
as an illumination,
as a shield and protection,
in the heart of the city did he set it.
For which let us sing to the Immaculate Virgin:
Rejoice, oh dwelling and home of Christ our God;
Rejoice, oh vessel of His ineffable glory.
Rejoice, oh city quickened in spirit, reigning forever.
Rejoice, oh brightly embellished chamber.
Rejoice, oh Joy of cities and villages.
Rejoice, oh invincible refuge and fortress of Christians in
 distress.
Rejoice, oh glory of the Orthodox Church.
Rejoice, oh affirmation of the Russian land.
Rejoice, oh Helper of the Christ-loving army.
Rejoice, oh conquest of our enemies.
Rejoice, oh deliverance from misfortune.
Rejoice, oh Thou who visitest on all Thy maternal bounties.
Rejoice, oh zealous Intercessor for the Christian race.

XXIII

Soviet Information Bureau, late December 1941:

Evening bulletin, 22 December
Over the course of 22 December, our forces engaged adversaries in combat on all fronts. In several sectors of the WESTERN, KALININ, SOUTHWESTERN, AND LENINGRAD fronts, our forces, engaging in fierce fighting with the enemy, continued to make headway and took a number of populated areas.

26 December (within the last hour)
During the period from December 18 to 25, units of Major-General Comrade Fedyuninsky's 54th Army (Leningrad Front) crushed the Volkhov group of enemy forces. As a result of this group's destruction, we captured the following trophies of war: artillery pieces: 87, heavy machineguns: 47, hand-held machineguns: 166, automatic carbines: 57, rifles: 600, tanks: 26, mortars: 142, cargo trucks: 200, cartridges: more than 300,000, mines: 13,000, grenades: 10,000, bicycles: 400, and a large amount of other matériel. 6,000 German soldiers and officers were killed.

32 populated areas were liberated from the enemy.

27 December (within the last hour)
In battles with the German invaders from December 17 to 27, the forces of the Kalinin Front CAPTURED the following trophies of war: tanks and tankettes: 103, armored vehicles: 6, artillery pieces of various calibers: 180, machineguns: 267, automatic carbines: 135, mortars: 86, flamethrowers: 6, rifles: 659, motor vehicles: 1,323, motorcycles: 348, bicycles: 213, airplanes: 8, radio sets: 6, carts: 115, horses: 130, shells: 12,200, landmines of various calibers: more than 8,300, rifle cartridges: 778,480, grenades: 1,270, and other matériel.

332 populated areas were liberated from the German invaders.

30 December (within the last hour)

On December 29 and 30, the Caucasian Front forces, in conjunction with the naval forces of the Black Sea Fleet, launched an assault on the Crimean Peninsula and after stubborn hostilities occupied the city and fortress of KERCH and the city of THEODOSIA.

In both sectors the enemy is in retreat, pursued by our units. Trophies of war have been captured and are being tallied.

Chapter Four
UNDER THE SIGN OF
ALPHA AND OMEGA

XXIV

At the beginning of January, the city was plunged into total darkness and starvation, the air raids and artillery bombardments stopped, and all work came to a halt.

Only now, after four months of siege, did Gleb fully realize that he was not simply a witness to a battle fought against a pack of ravening wolves, whose reason had been clouded long before by a false sense of their own exclusivity and the "pure breeding" of their pack (which purity was entirely illusory). It turned out that what was taking place was a clash between two vital energies: one, having broken adrift from the foundations, was seeking a meaning, a secret code, in the workings of the incomprehensible and supposedly hostile world of the opposing force, those "others," who thought and lived in close proximity to the primary source, in calm possession of knowledge. It was an attempt to burgle the sacred treasure chest of Russian life, a Faustian urge to push insatiable curiosity to its limit, a craving nourished by a strange desire that exceeded the bounds of everything essential to human nature, the desire to press—over and over again—the question of what lay beyond the ultimate boundary: a conquistadorial, cunning, serpentine craving that poisoned all under its sway, compelling them to annihilate those "others" in order to find out why they behaved as they did, why they "weren't like everyone else," and to repeat the terrible experiment over and over again; it was a craving that gave birth to monsters and cannibals. And Petersburg now appeared to Gleb as what it had always been, covertly, in secret—the focused potential of the energies of the whole of Russia, the embodiment of its indomitability and tranquil understanding of both past and future, its understanding of man as opposed to nature and of the inherent nature of the human being. Petersburg and Russia had no need to search for "keys"—those had been given from the outset. And Gleb suddenly remembered that he had heard similar thoughts expressed twenty years earlier by the Chetvertinskys. Fyodor, Sergei's older brother, was fond of repeating: "It's all in the language." And this language has been given to us from birth; it only needs to be used correctly—that was what Gleb thought now. The Finns, adventitious fellow travelers of the rabid pack, have shown no sign of any real commitment. Although we have different roots, in their soul they are closer to us. But the pack does have its allies—investigators of Russian nature under the banner of a universal experiment, of "the worldwide Soviet Union" (as the words of their anthem have it). If Petersburg falls and Leningrad triumphs, it will be a joint victory for them—for these somber wolves, these Fausts and their hammer-and-sickle Wagners. Gleb realized that for the first time, in thinking of the Soviets, he had said—if only to himself—not "we," but "they" and "them." But experience had given him that right.

XXV

From Gleb's notebook:

6 January 1942. Christmas (Old Style)
Impressions from an afternoon "stroll":

by the Summer Garden,

an abandoned corpse, wrapped in sackcloth,
felt boots protruding, string untwined.
I see—from the figure—that it's a woman.
Then another abandoned corpse,
another and another,
but that one's barefoot,
and this one, in long-nosed shoes,
dropped right here on the bridge,
just as he walked, hands in pockets,
and fell on his back—that's the way
they fall when they die
(yes, yes, heart failure).
Striding up, sheepskin-coated,
an officer of the law saw
the closed eyes and breathless mouth,
and went on his way.
Past a crowd of people—
some in overcoats
or padded work jackets,
others in fur coats,
dragging little sleds—mostly empty—
or carrying cans
or empty-handed,
with empty stomachs,
and empty, unfeeling hearts,
with gazes that have collapsed inward.
And there's a blind man striding along,
feeling out the way with a cane.
He checked the lying man
with his fingers and moved on.

If I were Sologub-and-Hippius,
with their homegrown Nietzscheism,

I would write something like this:

Burn, you accursed books!

XXVI

From Vera's diary:

Starvation ages.

All the fat is burned out. There's nothing left but skin, bones, and muscles—in men. It's easier on us women, we have more deposits and folds of fat, and so the aging is not so catastrophic. Even so, I try not to look at my reflection.

All that dieting and dreaming of a slim figure—how absurd! What wouldn't I give now for those pies and cakes, whipped cream, absolutely anything! But what's most terrible is Gleb's condition. He was thin enough before—all skin and muscles—and now he is covered in wrinkles, folds, hollows. The body can still be concealed under clothes, but the face! And the hands! It's as if he has put on about twenty-five years. Only the eyes are like before, so alive, inflamed with blazing youthfulness. As long as they still gleam like that, everything is all right.

He says he doesn't see that I have aged, but I can see him, and gazing into this "mirror," I realize what has happened to us.

XXVII

From Gleb's notebook:

January 13. New Year's Eve, 1942, Old Style.
-35⁰ C, not snowing, but with a light breeze.
A chronicle of the battle with cold:
first I went to Krestovsky Island,

with everyone else, to dismantle
the wood-plank stands
of the snow-covered stadium,
reminiscent of a crater
pockmarked all over from the dancing
of elephants or rhinoceroses.
I took some on the sled to Vera's place
(she helped as well),
and then, across Lieutenant Schmidt Bridge,
under shelling, I dragged some back to mine.
The planks are all burned up at last,
the stadium completely dismantled
by herds of hoar-frosted
human ants.
Back in the early winter,
before I acquired the planks—
which, alas, did not last long—
I started burning books for heat.
I burned: *Soviet Music*
          then Goethe in German,
          then Shakespeare in translation,
          then originals,
          then a cheap Pushkin
          (the Marx edition, I know
          it all by heart anyway)
          then a multivolume,
          commemorative Count Tolstoy—
          All these I regretted,
          but now life is dictating
          a different *War and Peace*.
          And then came Dostoevsky's turn—
          The Adolescent and *Poor People*.
I postponed for a while the burning

of *The Karamazovs*, *The Devils*, and *At Tikhon's*
(the Grossman edition).
When I threw *The Adolescent* into the stove,
I thought: "There it goes,
the final Russian paean
to Europe's 'sacred stones,'"
up in flames and smoke.
Not even stones will be left.
The survivors are: a little poetry
             (Blok, Arsenii Tatishchev),
             Latin incunabula,
             music scores, letters, a stack
             of music paper,
             heavy drawing paper
             and empty, unlined notebooks—
             they burn worst of all.
While I was writing, I've warmed up.
Let us call it "Vers la flamme."

XXVIII

More and more often, standing for hours at a time, waiting for
a delivery of food to arrive, Gleb witnessed a scene that recurred
with unvarying regularity—women, mostly elderly, reveling in
their own impunity and openly reviling the military and civil
authorities, to the morose approval of the utterly exhausted
queue, which eventually turned its eyes away (later they stopped
even turning their eyes away), and the clear indifference of the
forces of law and order, once so formidable. The militiamen,
who usually kept sentry duty at the empty grocery stores, either
pretended not to hear the bitter harangues or ostentatiously
moved off to one side. Words that during the first months of the
war were regarded as grounds for arrest and possible execution

by firing squad no longer made any impression. Because every second person, if not two out of every three, was prepared to utter them, as they stood in line for the bread that was so hard to chew up and the almost inedible oilseed meal, or as they crowded around the shops in the impossible hope that perhaps today they would announce at least the distribution of some kind of grain or—as at New Year's—even some sweet stuff. But, strangely enough, although Gleb acknowledged the subjective truth of what was being said about the appallingly, treacherously inadequate provisioning of the besieged city, about the complete lack of respect by the citizens and authorities for their own lives, about the excessive acquiescence and servility of those people who, by their mere presence in the city, bolstered the morale of our army and its determination to stand firm until victory, about the people's trampled dignity, he did not sympathize with these outbursts. Those female orators were spewing out their hatred of the deliberate or unwitting brutality and bestial oppression that had become a commonplace, in an attack on those who were now responsible for redeeming the almost catastrophic situation. And had not these same female orators only recently demanded, with hate in their hearts, reprisals against the genuine or imaginary opponents of their oppressors—with that same unspoken but crushing approval from the crowd that turned its eyes away? The word that Gleb used to himself was precisely that, "oppressors"; he had been aware of his own total alienation from the authorities for a long time already. But more important now was a different hate—and a different love, not the one that moved the crowd. His thoughts were interrupted by the familiar invective . . .

"Filthy, barbarian way of doing things, a stinking, rotten life. And we still trust these skunks and gangsters. They force us to live in terror and starvation and die up to our necks in sewage. The toilets are boarded up, everyone craps in the hallways or in the broken trams, even out in the street. Tell me, citizen, where did you relieve yourself today?"

"I've got a pass to the Hermitage. One of the halls there, you know, where the Dutch masters used to hang, has been sprinkled with fine sand, so it was all quite civilized really," the man accosted by the female orator answered imperturbably, even with a certain bravado.

"Wretched, lousy, stinking country, drowning in ignorance, hunger, and shit, living up to its knees in its blood and puke, breathing air saturated with the stink of corpses and believing that everyone else in the world envies it!"

A haggard militiaman, struggling to maintain at least some semblance of stern authority, walked over to the female orator.

"What's the problem, little lady?"

"Now what, do you think I'm crazy, traumatized? That people like me ought to be shot?" the woman carried on babbling, staring fiercely into the face of this representative of authority, whose mere appearance was enough to arouse sympathy: deeply sunken eyes, a hunger-furrowed face that could have belonged to a man of any age, a greatcoat dangling loosely on his massive frame, eyes glazing over from malnutrition.

"It's the doctors' job to decide who's traumatized. Anyway now, you be on your way . . . There won't be any bread today, citizens. And there won't be any grain either. Nothing at all is being issued today. Go on home in peace . . ."

It was dark—and he had to get home before the curfew. Another mind-numbing night of aching hunger.

XXIX

From Gleb's notebook:

January 15:

The important thing is not to eat
    dirty old paste from the wallpaper, nothing boils out of it;
        belts—they're treated with some kind of chemical—
    it isn't rawhide, like
the polar explorers used to boil up,
and not to eat the strange meat jelly sold on the black market.
God knows, what if it's boiled out of corpses from the nearest
    cemetery?
Or rather, the cemetery that is everywhere now.
Vera said fifty bodies have been left where they lie, littering
the freezing halls of the Hermitage.
Better diarrhea and vomit than losing one's mind.
Better the aching hunger . . .
    Although it's not really any better.

XXX

It was precisely in one of these moments of ultimate bodily humiliation—for the hunger was, first and foremost, humiliating—and despair, nudging him toward the void of nonexistence, that Gleb suddenly sensed that within him, too, there was a certain power at variance with the forces acting all around him, and this power was pushing its way out of the former Gleb Alpha like a spring. Perhaps it is the voice of blood and race that has begun speaking in me, as they are so fond of repeating in their propaganda—those who condemn me to death, together with hundreds of thousands of my compatriots caught in the trap of the siege: the call of the sun and the south.

Everything I wrote, everything I said and did before was wrong, because my view of things was distorted. Now I see clearly through a glass that is no longer cloudy. Now my view is bright. It encompasses the ends and the beginnings of things—everything accommodated in the span from A to Z. "I" used to be the point of departure, the "alpha" of a meaning, granted to me in its fullness only during these terrible months. Now I, Gleb Alfani, know how to respond to the challenge thrown down to me.

His thoughts felt cramped—Gleb was thinking about everything at once, keying himself up internally to a point at which the transient became eternal. Exactly two hundred years earlier, Bach had tempered his own clavier well. But Gleb Alfani's rebelliously free-spirited Russian and vibrantly mellifluous Italian soul resisted this global Germanic tempering. The world could not be tempered like that. No matter how liberal the constitution of intelligible space might be, and the bill of rights for sounds tied to a five-line stave, they left out of the picture everything that was tremulous, spontaneous, inexpressible in words. Vera, *verissima*—Gleb's childhood Italian, used only for reading comments on scores, was surfacing into consciousness again—had fallen in love with precisely this nameless quality pulsating within him.

What I am composing in my mind will be an anthem of overcoming. Not triumphal, no, but tremulous: like the voice of an evening prayer, like the conversation of those who love, like a premonition of victories to come. But not yet the victories themselves.

Let the underlying beat be set by the rhythm of the E-flat minor prelude from the first volume of *The Well-Tempered Clavier*. We shall accept the obvious: no one has ever set pitches to rhythm as well as that sage of Leipzig. But in its genuine pulse, the corporeal vestment of sounds must elude its own temperament. And so we shall take three instruments—three violas, three stringed violets with swords of resonant flame carved into their wooden bodies. (Where can they be obtained in a besieged city? Never mind, we'll ask the museum people.) The viola da gamba—the "knee violet"—with its body clasped between the knees. "I kiss your knees to stop the pain," Vera had told him in an insane note placed in his pocket before a brief separation in the autumn following the first terrible air raids. The viola da braccio—the "arm violet"—blossoming into sound in the embrace of the arm: "I shall press my lips against your shoulder for luck." The viola d'amore—the "violet of love"—the most tremulous and tender of the three, its neck, crowned by a carved wooden head with blindfolded eyes, lying in the palm of the hand. As a sign of love's heedless impulse. "I kiss your hand on the palm." Let their trio sing and pulse, like Gleb's body, arranged for three voices.

Let us call it "In This You Shall Conquer"—ἐν τούτῳ νίκα—(in) hoc (signo) vince(s).

Then they will be joined by a countertenor. Not a man and not a woman, but a voice transcending the limits of human embarrassment, located beyond the bounds of the corporeal, in a space of purity and precision that is entirely disembodied. We Italians previously entrusted this sort of thing to a special breed of mutilated nightingales, impotent in the simple, direct, male sense, and yet acquiring plenitude of expression through their mutilation. These days, following the rejection of that operation on the organ that arouses—in me, as in others—so much darkness, the torment of jealous, egotistical desire unilluminated by the kind of love that Vera and I have, kept secret from others and truly boundless only for us—these days such a part is normally sung by a countertenor, the most difficult range of all, the most unmasculine and unfeminine. But only the countertenor can transform the tone of the underlying substance of what I am now composing—the ardor of desire—and manifest it as a stream of lambent, limpid rays of light.

XXXI

"Verochka, I've begun writing an aria. It is suffused through and through with thoughts of you and our destiny. The piece will be in four voices—three violas and one countertenor. While I am working on it, I feel that nothing bad will happen to you or to us. That there is some invisible shield protecting us. But you must not stay on Vasilievsky any longer. Even though the place is never bombed or shelled. Why bother with these conventions?"

"I can't move into your place. I don't have just myself to think about."

"I understand, I should have spoken to Georgii a long time ago."

"It's not about Georgii. I'm pregnant."

"I told you, I should have spoken to your husband. A long time ago."

"What for? I'm pregnant, Gleb. And what kind of husband is he to me?"

"Whose child is it?"

"Yours. Who else's?"

"But why, why, why didn't you leave the city when it was still possible, then?"

"I was pregnant. It's four month now already. Four long months, Gleb."

"I can't leave you on Vasilievsky."

"You'll have to put up with it."

"I'm taking you away."

"Where to? Where you are, the shelling never stops. If not for the flak cannon by St. Isaac's, they'd bomb you too. Better find some milk."

"They keep cows in sheds on Ligovsky Prospect by Rastannaya Street. The dairymen aren't interested in incunabula and rare manuscripts. But I've still got a small Persian carpet left, and a pair of Chinese vases made to order for the emperor. You remember the ones—funny potbellied things with a warrior on horseback spearing a tiger? I got them as faulty goods because of the tiger. The Chinese have too much respect for dragons."

"Gleb, it's not just for me that we need the milk."

"I think they'll take the carpet, although the path down to the sheds is strewn with the things. Or the vases. Tomorrow Mark and I will load them up on the sled and try our luck."

"Just get some milk, please."

XXXII

As Gleb made his long way back along Nevsky Prospect with a huge, hermetically sealed churn of freezing milk from the Ligovka (Mark had got hold of the churn for him), the reddish sun, blurred by the deepening cold, hung in the giddy, vertiginous air without setting, as if refusing to accept that the frosty chill shackling the final remnants of consciousness and scrubbing the city and the faces of passersby completely white, had been augmented by a keen northeasterly that had sprung up again, intensifying the cold to the very limit of the bearable. "Even in the sun, with no wind, the thermometer shows minus thirty-four degrees. Today, January 24, the standard ration allowance has been increased . . ." Gleb started scraping out in his notebook with a pencil (the ink had frozen long ago), but then the will to write started to abandon him. In Gleb's perception the dull redness of the midday sun acquired a mystical tinge. That was probably how the lamp of heaven ought to look as time finally froze and came to a halt. At the point where Alpha fuses with Omega. Sitting there in the safety of the minimal warmth given out by the little stove, he pictured himself still standing in the windy street with the container of milk and staring fixedly at the unfading celestial luminary above the Gulf of Finland.

"Φώς ιλαρόν αγίας δόξης αθανάτου Πατρός, ουρανίου, αγίου, μάκαρος, Ιησού Χριστέ" thought Gleb, starting to recall something he had once learned by heart almost as a joke; and then, switching to another sacred language, in which his forebears used to pray, he continued to himself, "*Fulgor diei lucidus solisque lumen occidit, et nos ad horam vesperam te confitemur cantico.*" The winged luminary that seemed to be flooding the space of his awareness with light was the point of separation from everything onerous and dispiriting, the point of transfiguration and the attainment of a final, clear state of knowing. In precisely this way ". . . having come to the setting of the sun and beheld the light of evening," and rising above Calamity and Grief, rising above Valor, for this new sun was even greater than Valor, Victory, and Faith, we shall sing in praise of "God, Father, Son, and Holy Spirit. For meet it is at all times to worship Thee with voices of praise. O Son of God and Giver of Life, therefore all the world doth glorify Thee." That was precisely how the voice personifying all the living should proclaim its praise in the sacred tongues known to Gleb Alfani's heart, in his final and most important composition, born under the sign of the beginning and the end, Alpha and Omega. Now everything was falling into place.

Chapter Five
THE TABLE OF KINGS

XXXIII

Top Secret
10 February 1942

The situation with foodstuffs in Leningrad remained difficult in January and early February.

The population's ration cards were not fully redeemed against the January norms for meat, fats, and confectionery goods.

Of the monthly requirement for fats due to be issued against ration cards in January, of 1,362 tons, 889 tons were not issued to the population.

Of 1,932 tons of meat specified for issue, 1,095 tons were not issued.

Of the 2,639 tons of confectionery goods that should have been issued against cards in January, 1,379 tons were not issued to the population.

As a result of the food supply difficulties and the lack of water, light, and fuel in the housing sector, the negative mood of the population is not diminishing . . .

	December 1941	January 1942
Births	5205	4310
Deaths	52612	96751

In recent days, mortality has increased sharply in the city. In ten days of February, 36,606 people have died.

Of these, during the same period, 1,060 people died suddenly on the streets of the city. In those ten days, there were twenty-six cases of murder and robbery with intent to take possession of food products and food rationing cards . . .

There has been a sharp increase in the number of reported cases of cannibalism, and especially the use of cadavers in food. In just ten days in February, 311 people were arrested for cannibalism in the city of Leningrad and its suburban areas.

In all, 724 people have been arrested for these crimes.

Of this number of arrestees, forty-five died in prison, mostly those individuals who had used cadavers as food. Cases against 178 people have been completed by investigators and forwarded to the Military Tribunal for consideration: 89 people have already been shot.

Commandant of the Leningrad District NKVD
Comissar of State Security, 3rd rank
Kubatkin

XXXIV

The milk that Gleb procured didn't last for long. It couldn't have lasted for long. It was clear to Vera that for the time being Gleb could carry on exchanging his property for food for her and their future child—her conscience wouldn't allow her to touch the things in the apartment where she had lived for several years with Beklemishev (it wasn't the act of deception itself that made her feel ashamed, only the fact that it would inevitably be exposed later on)—but this barter trade of Gleb's would have to come to an end sometime. The instinct of a mother, of the second, renewed Vera within the former Mrs. Beklemisheva—my God, was there really a time when I was proud of that name?—told her it would be safer to leave the besieged city via the ice road across frozen Lake Ladoga, which was operating well, and then travel on via train to the Volga region. And then things could take their course. In any case, the fact that she was pregnant by another man would come out eventually, but in order to save the child, even this was acceptable. The other option would have been to remain with Gleb, whom she loved infinitely, but who was borne along in the general stream and had failed to slice boldly through the knot of their situation—yes, yes, their situation, not hers alone!—and doing that would condemn her, the child, and Gleb to a slow but inevitable end among a wilderness of ruins.

And Vera began packing for the journey. She would leave the city very soon, without informing Gleb (for his own good, for *their* common good, and the salvation of *their* child), taking with her only what was absolutely necessary; but she decided to send Gleb the key to the Vasilievksy Island apartment through Mark—afterward, Gleb and Georgii could talk everything out between them, and Gleb would collect the rest of Vera's things, which would come in useful to him in bartering for food. She intended to send Gleb a letter explaining everything. Before she left, she had to stock up on clothes warm enough for the many hours needed to cross the lake, and food for the early stages of the onward journey. And Vera decided to exchange the personal effects that she didn't really need for food at the flea market.

XXXV

From Vera's diary:

February 15, 1942

Now, Gleb, I want to write something that concerns only the two of us. If we survive this horror, or even if one of us survives, for instance, only you, simply because your death is impossible for me to imagine, you will read this entry.

Know that I have loved, do love, and will love you with all my
heart.

With the whole sky, though it be clouded over.

With the sun, though it make only rare appearances.

With the air, filled once again with the mind-numbing
detonations of shells.

I love you with the blinding shroud of snow that separates us.

I love you with death.

With all my hope for life—and not only for my own.

Amo te plurimum ergo sum. You see, my education is good for
something.

Amo te plurimum ergo sum.

Amo te plurimum ergo sum.

XXXVI

Meanwhile, the talk of cannibalism, at first muted and then more
and more widespread, was confirmed by new facts. While Fyodor
Stanislavovich Chetvertinsky was occupied with a poor excuse
for scholarly work—it could not be called genuine work—as well
as efforts to obtain rations and firewood for his extremely aged
and infirm colleagues, and also to rescue extremely rare books
and materials from places pierced by artillery shells, be they
private apartments or the premises of the Academy of Sciences
itself, thereby earning his wife's and his own daily bread in the
form of academic supplements to their hideously scanty rations,
Evdokiya Alexeevna helped him by exchanging all the more or
less unnecessary things in their home for food at the flea market,
and standing for hours at a time in the exhausting queues for
food, from which she returned with more and more depressing
news and impressions. As he moved about in the center of the
city, Chetvertinsky tried not to look around him, but some of
the things his wife reported dented even his sangfroid. No one

let their children out for walks on their own any longer, not even to go to school (if classes were still being given). At the next entrance to their building, where the massive, carved street doors had been torn off by a bomb blast, a gang of people driven insane by hunger had tried to smash in the door of an apartment with axes in broad daylight: a three-year-old little girl and a six-year-old boy were locked away inside until their parents came back. But either the door had proved too well made—it was a tenement building from 1910–1912, in which the Chetvertinskys had once owned a share, and during the housing "consolidation" of the early 1920s the authorities had shown them some consideration, allowing Fyodor Stanislavovich to carry on living there in a mediocre apartment—or else the officers of the law summoned by the neighbors (the children were terrified out of their minds) had arrived in the nick of time. Sometimes Evdokiya Alexeevna told him absolutely incredible things: that morning, on the 24th anniversary of the Red Army and Navy—in whom can we place our hopes now, if not them?—she thought she had seen the freshly severed head of an exceptionally pretty young woman on the blinding, glittering snow near the Tauride Garden, and somehow it had reminded her of Vera Beklemisheva, with the same short hairstyle that Vera had, and there were bloody underclothes and warm stockings lying beside it. The body had obviously been "put to good use."

"My God, Dusya, pull yourself together, don't say such things. And what would Beklemisheva be doing around here anyway? She lives in the middle of Vasilievsky Island. You must be mistaken."

"It's such a terrible thought, Fedenka, but what if she was going to the flea market to barter something, and they lured her in somewhere and . . . It's too terrible to think about. Poor Georgii!"

"Well, firstly, they have their own flea market there. And secondly, I heard she'd fallen out with Beklemishev and supposedly taken up with Gleb Alfani, and he lives over on Labor Square. So there's absolutely no reason for her to be here."

"It's so terrible to think about it, absolutely terrible."

After this talk Chetvertinsky nonetheless took a walk to the Tauride Garden, not a long journey, but exhausting. His festive mood—they had announced on the radio that white-collar workers and their dependents were to be issued a ration of cocoa over and above the norm—had evaporated. Naturally, he didn't find any traces of anyone's morning—or evening?—feast; well, except for patches of frozen blood in several places by the railings, which was quite normal in view of the constant shelling. But the severed head and, especially, the clothes could have been taken by someone: the clothes to be resold, and the head—it really was better not to think about it—for jellied meat. "My wife's health has been badly affected, including her mental state," Chetvertinsky told himself. Evdokiya Alexeevna's psychological well-being—the essential condition of her survival—what was concerned him most of all now.

"You imagined it, Dusya," he told his wife firmly when he got home, then held out the little carton of powder he'd picked up in a shop and added, "Let's brew some cocoa."

PART THREE:
SPRING

Chapter Six
THREE SEASONS OF DEATH

XXXVII

From the very beginning of the siege, the two main floating fortresses of the Red Army's Baltic Fleet—the battleship *Marat* and the cruiser *Kirov*—cruised in the proximity of the Neva estuary, as if symbolizing the two phases of the Revolution. The *Marat*, which took up position beside Kronstadt and fired from there with all the might of its 305-millimetre guns at the German forces advancing along the southern shore of the Gulf of Finland, was a reminder of the time when the Revolution had decked itself out in the garb of a sanguinary but philosophically enlightened minority, who had slaughtered a quarter of the country out of logical necessity—those who survived would hold sway over a new earth, in a new heaven; while, the *Kirov*, the flagship and HQ of the Baltic Fleet at the time of Tallinn's evacuation, having moved into the estuary and moored at the 19th line of Vasilievsky Island, firing over the city blocks from there, served as a reminder of the phase of temporary restraint, of Jacobinism, of radicalism in words but not in deeds, of the Soviet "imposition of order" that was cut short by the shot in a corridor of the Smolny Institute that ended Kirov's life on the first of December, 1934. This was, so to speak, the official version of events, differing greatly from the Revolution as seen by Gleb, the Chetvertinskys, and many others who either accepted it or did not accept it. But as long as both floating fortresses, together with the battleship the *October Revolution*, cruised between Kronstadt and the besieged city, the city was content with this version.

During the final third of September the Germans attacked the *Marat* from the air with devastating force, destroying its forward turret, powder magazines, and wheelhouse. Badly crippled and with a third of its combat personnel killed, it was stuck on the shoals off Kronstadt, but continued firing from the barrels of its remaining guns, while the *Kirov* and the *October Revolution* took refuge in branches of the Neva, merging into the residential areas that were being destroyed, together with their dying palace complexes and parks. The heroic story of the Soviet coup was replaced by a different narrative, far less exalted and immeasurably more terrible—of the reduction of everything still endowed with any meaning to a heap of rubble, to obscurantist gibberish.

"A lousy, stinking city, as cramped as a rear entrance cluttered with garbage, is the only thing left to us, and this is not Petersburg," Gleb began the latest entry in his notebook, but the fervid heat of his constantly rising excitement, and what he had taken for a new, clearer view of things, proved, alas, to be plain, ordinary flu, extremely dangerous to a starving man. Gathering the remnants of his will into a tight fist, Gleb forced himself to swallow the anti-catarrhal medicine and aspirin he had been keeping in reserve, as well as a certain quantity of homoeopathic pills. Tormented by a splitting headache, drifting in and out of unconsciousness, Gleb remembered—or did he dream it?—Mark coming by and saying he had brought extremely important news, but being unable to bring himself to tell Gleb what it was and just sitting there for a long time and finally leaving some keys behind when he went. Gleb could have accepted that there had never been any visit from Nepshchevansky, that it was his mind's defensive reaction against the vortex that was sucking it in, except for the keys—there they were, lying in the room on the lid of the grand piano. Beside them Gleb discovered an opened letter, sent by the internal municipal post, postmarked February 20, 1942. In the letter, Vera explained the reasons for her sudden evacuation and informed Gleb that she had also written to Georgii, and "when, in a month or month and a half you receive word from me that I have safely reached the Volga Region, I ask you to go around to the apartment, after first contacting Georgii, and collect the things that I will indicate in my next letter. Don't bother any sooner, there is no need. May the powers on high preserve you. I kiss you, my beloved. Yours to the grave, Vera." Thus the mystery of the keys was solved. But what was it that Mark had wanted to tell him? Stunned by the letter in his weakened state, Gleb was certain that the extraordinary news must concern Vera's departure, but there was no way he could contact Mark. No one answered the phone in Nepshchevansky's apartment, and the Leningrad office of TASS informed him that Mark had been out of the city for several days.

XXXVIII

PRIEST:
> Let God arise,
> let his enemies be scattered—

CHORUS:
> Christ is risen from the dead,
> trampling down death by death,
> and on those in the grave
> bestowing life.

PRIEST:
> As smoke vanishes,
> so let them vanish—

(*The CHORUS repeats the troparion of the Feast of Easter.*)

> So the sinners will perish

before the face of God,
but let the righteous be glad.

(*The CHORUS repeats the troparion.*)

This is the day which the Lord has made,
let us rejoice and be glad in it!

(*The CHORUS repeats the troparion.*)

Glory be to the Father and the Son and the Holy Spirit—

(*The CHORUS repeats the troparion.*)

Now and forever, until the end of time, amen.

(*The CHORUS repeats the troparion.*)

PRIEST:
Christ is risen from the dead,
trampling down death by death,

CHORUS:
and on those in the grave
bestowing life.

Gleb had known the melody and voice parts of this triumphant hymn by heart since he was a little child, from the first time he was taken to a midnight vigil, merging into a long, four-hour matins, but not until his juvenile years did he learn that the hymn's music was written by the composer of *Askold's Grave*—the godfather, in a certain sense, of the last of the Radziwiłłs—and that this composer, Alexei Verstovsky, had been, like Askold, like

Savromatov, and like Gleb himself, agonizingly torn between the basic, elemental, magic of the language he imbibed with his mother's milk and its setting in a hymn of praise transcending spontaneous elementality, "The Sun that was before the sun and Who had once set in the tomb . . ." as the Easter *ikos* said.

The imperative of recovery, thoughts of salvation, and Vera jostled with each other in his agitated awareness. But now that Vera was far away, Gleb could at least place the final dot in the music of the aria with a clear conscience.

XXXIX

The bombing raids and artillery bombardments were especially intense on Easter eve. Despite an immense desire to go to church, which had been growing insistently since Evdokiya Alexeevna left him, Chetvertinsky decided not to take the risk, knowing what a long and dangerous road it was. From early in the morning the guns fired their rumbling shots, sparsely and methodically, with a maddening regularity, in time to his own slowed heartbeat. Five minutes before seven in the evening, when Orthodox Christians prepare themselves inwardly, mentally, for the midnight service, reciting prayers, and the Liturgy of St. Basil the Great begins in the churches, there was an air-raid siren, and the buildings in the part of the city where Fyodor Stanislavovich lived shuddered as the bombs dropped, scattering stone chips, structural debris, and glass from the windows that hadn't already been shattered. During the raid, the enemy's artillery carried on pounding the residential districts with the same loitering rhythm, sometimes coinciding ominously with the explosions of the bombs, sometimes generating a savage counterpoint. Massed, intensive return fire from our anti-aircraft guns—shooting up at targets invisible to the eye—as well as our own planes cleared the sky after an hour. When the curfew came into force, excluding the very idea of any

Procession of the Cross (although in a city shattered by bombs and flooded with blood and sewage, that would have been a powerful spectacle—if, that is, anything could still impress people after all that they had been through), Chetvertinsky, like many others, stayed awake until midnight, then broke his fast with the vodka he had been saving specially for Easter since it was issued as part of his academic ration, bundled himself up tight in the blankets that gave only a meager warmth, and lay down on his dirty bed without getting undressed. He had a good, warm feeling and felt less lonely. But no sooner did Fyodor Stanislavovich nod off than a new, even fiercer raid began, right on time for the Easter matins (the phosphorescent hands of the alarm clock showed one in the morning). The all clear for the city wasn't sounded until a quarter past three.

In the morning, the frosty, frozen streets were covered with new puddles of blood from the dead and wounded. So some people had defied the prohibitions and gone to church as twilight drew in after all. A cold wind was blowing from the gulf. The German heavy guns were still thumping in the same rhythm. The only planes that could be seen were ours—the enemy and his hellish legions were not in the sky on April 5, 1942, the day of Christ's Radiant Resurrection. The sight of the destruction and the large number of bodies in the streets on this cold day, which was nonetheless a holiday for many—although a working day in the Soviet calendar—was depressing. Aware of the German respect for precise schedules, Chetvertinsky was certain that the raid hadn't been improvised. He pictured to himself an air-force officer—somewhere in Tsarskoe Selo or Gatchina—who had invited a priest for a formal consultation, jotting things down in a notebook: "Evening service at seven, you say, in all the parishes? Procession of the Cross at midnight? And matins at one? Timber for heating the church buildings? Very well, we'll bear your wishes in mind. Please, have a coffee and a biscuit. What, today is a strict fast? Well, we respect the local customs." With someone else the same officer would have discussed the late quartets of Mozart. With Chetvertinsky he would probably have discussed linguistics, the common Indo-Aryan legacy—with insistent emphasis on the "Aryan" part—of our languages. This much-vaunted cultural veneer was merely the camouflage of an arrant cannibalism implanted by the victors even among the tribes they enslaved. Chetvertinsky shuddered once again at the thought of the suspicious meat jelly in the patties that were sold on the underground black market. It was easy to imagine the unbridled barbarity that would triumph if the absolutely inconceivable occurred—Fyodor Stanislavovich was more convinced than ever that it was inconceivable—and the National Socialists, these bards of tribal nirvana, were triumphant. The only point that still agitated the scholar's inquisitive mind was the stubborn rumors that had been circulating for several months concerning certain former acquaintances and students of his, who, finding themselves in the German zone, had sided with these crusaders against godless Bolshevism—a likelihood that could not be entirely ruled out, in view of how rapidly the enemy had overrun the outlying suburbs in August and September. "The German regime is every bit as godless as our own," Chetvertinsky told himself, "but we'll sort ours out after the war. All these people do is hammer away sadistically, day and night, at a city, the equal of which they could never hope to build; all they do is suffocate us slowly with the garrote of hunger and flood the streets with blood—and when, of all times? On the day of the Radiant Resurrection."

XL

As we walked past the Lithuanian Castle,
magnesium started flashing,
as if the clear, bright sun of August

was inadequate for the infamy
with which the entire ritual has been tainted
since the times when the bullheaded
God of the Neva's (Nile's) waters
was interred, hewn asunder:
the body, wrapped in the hieroglyphs of songs—
into the ground with it,
so that later,
in time's fullness,
it will splash forth
through harmonies agitating the air,
through rows of typesetter's lines
in a wind of numinous pages.

These lines from the second page of Tatishchev's *Lightsound* could only be a description of Blok's funeral.

Where was it, that Lithuanian Castle that was burned in the revolution? Gleb remembered so clearly the procession passing by its desolate walls on August 10, 1921. Where were those who walked along its walls, now that the entire city had become that Lithuanian Castle, an oppressive, dismal torture chamber, first erected on the shoulders and bones of Gleb's own generation, then burned and bombed to pieces in the hurricane wind of war; now that the rite of Egyptian burial, prophetically foretold from the year 1921, had become an everyday commonplace, and the lines of carts, sleds, or simple pieces of plywood with ropes tied to them—and with lifeless bodies, wrapped in sheets, lying on them—had stretched along broad October 25 Prospect for so many long months; now, when rumors of the ritual partial dismemberment of bodies had long ago ceased to alarm (Gleb himself had seen stacks of these mutilated, frozen bodies, with their thighs and other edible parts cut away—human beef for cannibals); precisely now, on the threshold of spring and a new blossoming, on the eve of the world's inevitable rebirth, Gleb began to realize the true scale of the collapse that had occurred, a collapse that made any past reality, even the most unendurable, seem like paradise. The wreck suffered by man this winter was total and irreversible—and his place had been taken by someone new, who had nothing in common with the beautiful city's former occupant aside from the details in his passport. And it must be admitted that Gleb himself dreaded this newfound trans-human power that now dwelt within him too. It wasn't physical, but a power of some other kind. What manifested itself at the physical level was a profound exhaustion from the flu he had suffered at the end of the hungry winter.

Radonitsa, the day of remembrance, arrived—the day on which, as Gleb's mother had taught him, one should visit the graves of one's parents. And Gleb set out to the devastated Vyborg Cemetery, where his father, Vladimir Georgievich, had been buried in 1915, and before that his grandfather, Giorgio Alfani. Gleb didn't remember his grandfather very well.

The site of the cemetery was now occupied by an iron foundry. The Gothic bell tower still thrust its pinnacle up into the sky. And although the guards kept squinting suspiciously at Gleb as he wandered along the factory wall that once bounded the cemetery, and there were only a few gravestones that had survived inside the wall, Gleb still managed to peer over it and make out the spot where his grandfather and father had once lain, and in his thoughts he asked God, if not to grant peace to their disturbed remains, then at least to make their inevitable meeting in *that place* a happy one. "But with Granddad I'll have to strain my knowledge of Italian to the limit. Oh, what nonsense! Does anyone really care what language you speak there?"

On April 15, the trams finally started running. It was time to fulfill the request Vera had made so long ago. In a strange way, the absence of news only reassured Gleb. It meant that all was well with Vera, that everything must definitely be well.

Early in the morning, Gleb got into a tram crammed to the very limit with people (it was route number 7), which ran through Labor Square and across Lieutenant Schmidt Bridge, with the steel colossus of the cruiser *Kirov* glinting a little distance away, then along Lieutenant Schmidt Embankment, and on along the 8th and 9th lines of Vasilievsky Island and Mussorgsky Prospect—how many times he had walked this way in the winter!—until it reached the tramline loop near the 24th and 25th lines, beside the tram depot. Vera had lived quite close by.

Ten minutes later he was already turning the key in the door of the Beklemishev residence (the electric bell still didn't work, and no one answered his knock), and a minute after that he was standing in the hallway. Everything was still just the way it had been, and it seemed as if Vera had only just gone out, although she hadn't been in the apartment for about two months. Lying beside the hallstand was a rather down-at-heel pair of women's winter shoes and several bundles, tied in thorough male fashion, of warm winter underclothes and other, lighter garments (Gleb noted to himself with the first stirrings of jealousy that only Georgii or Mark could have tied them up like that), as well as a little bundle of papers and two books. Simple items of makeup—a powder puff and pencils—had been left in front of the mirror. Gleb drew air in through his nostrils, catching a smell that definitely boded ill—the smell of rooms abandoned a long time ago, suddenly and in haste. He stepped into the living room, where a medium-sized canvas with orange hippopotamus-zebras and winged Cerberus-Semargls beside the Bank Bridge caught his eye, glittering in the rays of morning sunlight. Standing on the woven red-check tablecloth covering the table—from the Volga estate of Yulia Antonovna's father, as Vera had told Gleb during one of his evening visits here—was a half-drunk enamel mug of hot water that had frozen long ago. The handsome metal stove, acquired by Georgii Beklemishev at the beginning of autumn, was full of burned-out ash. No explanations were required. Now Gleb was certain that the news Nepshchevansky had brought for him was truly exceptional. But why, why, has this happened to me? Why has it happened to us? And why am I the last to find out about it?

How was Gleb to know that Beklemishev had been lying in one of the besieged city's hospitals for several weeks with a severe concussion? (The icebound ship in the Neva estuary, on which Georgii transcribed and translated the enemy's radio communications, had been shattered by intense bombing and shelling.) Or that Nepshchevansky had been killed by a sniper during a photo session at the Oranienbaum Bridgehead, and now there was no one left to hear the details from?

In the drawing room, Gleb lowered himself heavily onto a fine carved-wood chair that had somehow avoided being burned for heat during the winter, and sat there until twilight fell.

Chapter Seven
PRINCE TUMANOV

XLI

He was woven out of Baltic twilight mirages, out of whispers, out of the rustling of the wind in the torn sheets of iron and garbage, out of the sun that was red with cold, out of the illusory elevation— above the ruler-line streets—of those elemental images that chafed at Chetvertinsky's consciousness: horseman, flowing water, thunderstorms. He was woven in a fiery blast from the muzzles of guns aimed at the city from the south and the southwest, he came showering down as stone chippings and acrid smoke, condensing into the figure that Fyodor Stanislavovich had sensed behind him for several days now, on his way home from the Public Library to the building on Staronevsky Prospect, which had been damaged by a bomb, but was still habitable. Looking round, he saw this figure, with its light, elegant build and a military uniform that suited it well, fading into the crowd or crossing to the other side of the street in the blizzard. "There goes the traveling companion of my fears, the prince of my ravings," Fyodor Stanislavovich told himself. Sometimes an air-raid siren or the start of an artillery bombardment caught Chetvertinsky at the Anichkov Bridge, but a profound, inhuman exhaustion forced him either to ignore the danger completely and continue his impassive movement along the side of the prospect that was less dangerous during shelling— but equally fatal during an air raid—or else to stand under the first archway he came across on that side of Fontanka and wait until the bombs and shells stopped detonating: and then Chetvertinsky no longer sensed behind him the presence that had become his constant companion in recent days.

After he took his wife's body, sewn into an old sheet, to the Tauride Garden, now transformed into an immense morgue, on a little sled (he didn't have the strength to go as far as the cemetery), those people with whom he had unfinished discussions and arguments had suddenly started visiting him. Yesterday, for instance, he had distinctly heard the voice of a well-known Indologist behind him, objecting to Chetvertinsky's criticism of parallels between the Buddhist "flow" and intuitivism in Bergson's understanding of time. "But listen, Prince, Bergson is an absolute individualist, a Cartesian to the power of two," Chetvertinsky had replied, without turning round. "It's not for you or me, Prince, to sing the praises of the individual after everything that has happened. On the contrary, as men of the approaching post-human future, as men after the downfall of man . . ." He knew quite definitely that his interlocutor was no longer alive. He himself had just visited the man's apartment and sorted through his library before arranging its transfer to the archives of the Academy of Sciences.

April 16 turned out sunny. The mud and slush were drying out very quickly, although there were still heaps of uncleared garbage and sewage lying around everywhere. The previous day the trams had started running again, and the clanging of the moving carriages, forgotten over the dead winter, mingled with the song of the lark. "The bird of spring and life in our graveyard," thought Chetvertinsky. "What love is it seeking here, among the grief, the putrefaction, the stench?" Accustomed for so long to the firing of heavy guns, people walked along the streets with faces that expressed nothing but exhaustion. The first bothersome flies appeared. They roused an incomprehensible joy in Fyodor Stanislavovich's heart, and he didn't even brush them off his sleeves and face. Life in its very simplest, most ineradicable forms was awakening in powerful jolts, and his shattered heart, his soul desiccated by grief, his brain laid waste by hunger, and his stomach, too, all started vibrating in harmony with the fluttering of something already forgotten, but still as young as ever. Chetvertinsky was considerably surprised to spot a small flock of butterflies hovering over the pavement, but he simply could not recall the Latin name of their species. Everything sunny and placid had long ago retreated into a distant corner of his consciousness and only with the belated onset of the thaw had it started being blown back out. "I *will* remember, I will remember today," Fyodor Stanislavovich assured himself, but he didn't feel like thinking anymore. "Our poor Soviet Persephone has come to visit us from the kingdom of shadows"—this was the only thought that took shape in his mind.

More worn out than usual, Chetvertinsky leaned against the massive door of the apartment and reached into his deep coat pocket for the key, but the door yielded to the pressure of his body and opened slowly on its own. Having become accustomed over the winter to not being surprised by anything, Fyodor Stanislavovich stepped into the immense, empty corridor—almost everything that could be exchanged for food had been exchanged—and the dim mirror reflected a threadbare coat, a tattered scarf, and a dirty hat with earflaps set on the head of an untidily shaved, very thin man with inflamed eyes. After sliding a hostile glance over his own reflection, Chetvertinsky headed, without removing his hat or his shoes, for the kitchen, where someone was sitting and waiting, framed by the early evening light that filled the window, sipping hot water from Chetvertinsky's favorite glass with a quite unblockade-like, indeed rather foppish air—an athletically thin military man with a tan that certainly hadn't been acquired in the winter and the collar tabs of a lieutenant in the NKVD. Chetvertinsky couldn't immediately make out the uninvited guest's face, because the light from outside the window dazzled his eyes.

"Pardon me for intruding on your solitude," the stranger began.

"To what do I owe the pleasure?" Chetvertinsky asked tensely.

"Well now, Fyodor Stanislavovich, I am inexpressibly glad to see you. After all these years, you can't even imagine . . ."

"Is this an interrogation, or an arrest?" his host interrupted.

"Oh, come now."

"Then get to the point, please."

Chetvertinsky sat at the table with his back to the light. The cold of the street had just begun to release its grip, and he unbuttoned his coat. His guest was apparently insensitive to the temperature and had been sitting in the chill without a greatcoat. There wasn't even any steam coming out of his mouth, which only reinforced the dreamlike atmosphere. The lieutenant smiled broadly with his mouth and his eyes, and his trimmed moustache, combined with the dark hair slicked smoothly back, and a uniform that was still fresh, gave him a theatrical air. Chetvertinsky realized that he knew this young man—he had known him a long time ago, and very well, but between that life, in which they had associated and spoken at length and very productively, and the present life, there lay a massive glacial barrage of ineradicable cold, hunger, sewage, bloody diarrhea, shameful suffering, and death breathing down his neck.

"Iraklii, to what do I owe . . ."

"Indeed. Evening's coming on and we have a lot to talk over, Fyodor Stanislavovich. We probably won't get through it before curfew. Of course, I have a pass, but I'm free today, and if you'll permit me, I shall spend the night here."

"By all means, stay . . . Evdokiya Alexeevna died, her bed is free."

"This is pure alcohol. To her eternal memory!"

They drank without clinking glasses. The alcohol seared Chetvertinsky's throat and he almost choked.

"So then, you, Iraklii—that is, Iraklii Konstantinovich . . ."

"No superfluous formality, please, Fyodor Stanislavovich. Two days ago, did someone from the Academy of Sciences come to see you and tell you to expect an important visitor from Tashkent?"

"Something of the sort."

"Well, now here I am. On direct secondment from Central Asia. Across the lake on a truck. Along the ice road—the ice is still strong."

"I must confess I thought it was a matter of evacuation."

"In order to avoid unnecessary questions, allow me to introduce myself properly," said the visitor, taking out an identity document: it had been issued to a certain Iraklii Konstantinovich Nebulovich, seconded on special assignment to the command of the head of the Leningrad Region office of the NKVD, Commissar of State Security, third rank, Comrade Kubatkin.

"So you're a Ukrainian now?"

"Well, I didn't just appear out of the fog—or mist, or smoke, for that matter."

"I have heard various rumors, Iraklii."

"There's no smoke without fire, Fyodor Stanislavovich. Let's get to the point. We've read your letter to a colleague, and we liked a lot of what was in it. Especially your arguments concerning the Russian's closer relationship to his Indo-Aryan roots."

"Yes, but the letter wasn't even sent. I have only a vague idea of Professor Pokorny's whereabouts. Somewhere in Belgium, if I'm not mistaken . . ."

The visitor twirled an unsealed envelope in the tips of his fingers.

"You think we exiled Pokorny from Berlin because he's our enemy? In actual fact he is working with us, we share a common cause, and his non-Aryan origin is a matter of absolute indifference."

"Who are 'we'?"

"The German revolution needs people like you, Fyodor

Stanislavovich. We are completing the work begun by the Bolsheviks. Work for all, death to the cities, life on the free earth. The worker returns to a primeval paradise and becomes an Aryan tiller of the soil. We are the army defending him, you are the caste of wise priests. The Russian revolution, I think, also needs such people. Only our revolution is a complete turn: we carry things right through, beyond the limits of . . . hmm . . . economism. What do you say?"

"If this is a provocation . . ."

"Indeed not—or, if this is a provocation, then only in the very highest, nonmaterial sense. And then, I respect you too highly, your lectures opened my eyes to so many things that I couldn't possibly play such nonsensical games now. My struggle, our struggle—and everything that has happened since I disappeared from your field of view and joined the movement, the party, has been just such a relentless struggle—would have been impossible without the conviction that you planted in my mind. You are my true teacher."

"What is it that you want now, Iraklii?"

"Names, of course, Fyodor Stanislavovich," said the visitor, taking out a leather-bound notebook and a pencil. "But not only names. You and I are Russian men, and the Russian is always thinking of the future. Let me be frank: the general principles of the future world order are already clear. After our victory—in which I firmly believe—comes justice and, as I have already said, work for all, vengeance against the enemies of Aryan unity and the main culprits of the bungling Soviet regime, an improved standard of living, and the restoration of private property—how is it possible to work the land without that, to maintain an army and support you, the learned priests? And personal freedom. Of course a number of people will have to be shot or even hanged."

"I didn't teach you to shoot or hang people."

"What about the buffoons on the trees in your letter? We'll write them off as part of the inevitable overhead of war. The

German command has sent me to you on a special and, I would say, extremely delicate mission, concerning the formation of a new, free administration in the future exemplary center of Russia—in St. Petersburg."

"No more, that's enough." Chetvertinsky slammed his fist down on the table.

"Bear in mind," his visitor rebuked him calmly but rather crudely, tapping his fingernail on the NKVD identity document, "that this will be regarded as tantamount to refusal to cooperate."

"By whom, Iraklii?"

"By either side. Either of the two, Fyodor Stanislavovich. By speaking to me, you have already become an accomplice. After all, you won't go to the NKVD to complain about one of the Commissariat's officers, will you? And you're even less likely to complain to the German military authorities about their envoy. What's required of you at present is a mere trifle. Let's run through the list of the future government. They must be men who have demonstrably endured—blue-blooded and clearheaded. So: Prince Stcherbatsky."

"He died four weeks ago in Kazakhstan—he was evacuated there. I have absolutely reliable information to that effect."

The visitor made a mark in his little book.

"A great pity. A brilliant mind. True, he was fond of Bergson. We know about your differences of opinion. But comparing Kant with Buddhism is a mark in his favor. Beklemishev? I believe you thought very highly of him, when Georgii Vasilievich was still a student. They said he showed great promise."

"I've heard that Georgii has a domestic crisis on his hands."

"All the less to bind him to the past. We need men who are capable of action, not captive to emotion." The visitor continued his notes in the little book. "Gleb Alfani?"

"He was always a red."

"But we are also for justice. Don't you think that a sun symbol better suits the rock that Falconet's horseman has mounted, or the summit of Alexander's column, than the hammer and sickle?"

Chetvertinsky remained stubbornly silent.

"You yourself, Fyodor Stanislavovich Chetvertinsky. Prince Svyatopolk-Chetvertinsky."

"Oh, thank you most humbly."

"It's too late to back down: you already know everything. Complicity. Probably I should also be on the lists, and a number of other people noticed by the Germans, who work for them but are Russian at heart—after all, this is an allied administration. The young Baron von Ungern-Sternberg and Sonderführer Baron von Medem."

"This government is not turning out very Russian. We Svyatopolk-Chetvertinskys have intermingled with the Poles, and you, as I recall, Iraklii, are Georgian."

"Well, if Stalin can rule over the whole of Russia, what's wrong with the Tumanovs, relatives of the Bagrations and genuinely blue-blooded?"

"This is some kind of low farce," Chetvertinsky exclaimed in frustration.

"Please don't excite yourself, Fyodor Stanislavovich. You have already been of great help to us in any case. Whoever we might be. Here is your alibi," said the visitor, twirling the little book, gripped between his index and middle fingers. "Ah, yes, something that slipped my mind. Not so long ago I was in Paris and I met your brother there."

Chetvertinsky started.

"And, of course, you introduced yourself as Lieutenant Nebulovich?"

"Now why should I? As SS Untersturmführer Iraklii Tumanov. By the way, your brother has agreed to work for us."

"For whom?"

"You're probably curious for a glimpse of what your brother looks like now. I agreed to take a few photographs. You have to understand that this involved immense risk, but out of my boundless respect for you and what you did for me . . ."

"Don't bother."

"Your brother is just completing a new art-historical work—he told me it's the most important work of his life. It's called *A Hundred Years of Russian Glory*. He was a great friend of Gleb Vladimirovich's at one time, was he not? We would be glad to assist with the publication, but there are more urgent tasks for our common cause. We'll publish it at the end of this senselessly protracted . . ."

"All right, Iraklii, let me have the photographs."

"It's light already. Time I was going. I just can't seem to master the new tram routes . . . to go back in the direction of the Narva Gate. We have a safe passage there to Tsarskoye Selo."

"Then you need the number nine . . ."

As he stood on the corner of Volodarsky Prospect and October 25 Prospect on the oppressive, cloudy morning of April 17, watching the tram's reflection in the puddles that had frozen overnight as it set off toward Strikes Square, Fyodor Stanislavovich was still struggling to gather his wits after the night he had spent in discussion with a guest who had materialized so suddenly and equally suddenly melted away, like smoke, and therefore, to reinforce his spirits after the ordeal to which he had been subjected, he recited to himself: "As smoke vanishes, so let them vanish; as wax melts before the fire, so the sinners will perish before the face of those who love God and arm themselves with the sign of the cross . . ." Whoever his nocturnal visitor might have been, a protective prayer could do Chetvertinsky no harm.

Chapter Eight
LENINGRAD

XLII

Gleb's notebook:

April 20, 1942

It's warm outside, even hot, but the room and my heart are icy. Even the stove won't light: the smoke won't move from cold air to warm, and no amount of effort can warm me inwardly. And there's nothing that can be done about it.

What I am about to write is very important, and not just for me.

For a long time we thought that we were threatened by an external force—at first, a force of repression and tyranny, inducing fear, then a military force, striving overtly to exterminate, giving us no chance to take cover. We forgot that the enemy is not outside, but inside every one of us.

I, who at one time believed in the Revolution and welcomed it as the dawn of national and religious liberation, and spoke so much about all this during those delirious months with Sergei Chetvertinsky—about the inner kinship uniting many of us—and was then surprised that this impulse to blossoming was supplanted by soulless bureaucracy, and afterward, even when Sergei and Savromatov were already in Paris, continued to work stubbornly at connecting up the various strands of our musical, religious, and political thought (Nikander subsequently replied to a book of essays printed under the eye of the Revolutionary Military Censor with a sardonic letter from Paris: my dear Glebushka, he asked, why all this effort—one can write about all this or simply write the music. It's easy for him, he has the gift of genius as a composer, but he was not granted any capacity for sympathetic understanding)—even then I was aware that my soul was also clad in a gray greatcoat and soldier's leg wrappings, that it was there, with the indigent, homeless crowd of Red Army men sent to the slaughter, who in 1919 were left with the choice of dying or—if they held out—thwarting the triumph of the notorious opponents of our revolt. But were these militant opponents not themselves part of the revolt? It is terrible even to think what man of the center—the revolution was anything but the work of "men of the center"—would have come to power in a restoration of the heaven of the intelligentsia. And what a fierce blast would have ripped apart everything around it following that brief triumph!

We were what gave the forward impulse balance, a basis in memory and knowledge.

But then came the Young Communists. What did they know about the musty breath of restoration? And when they stopped our mouths and took the brakes off the flywheel of the revolution, the meat grinder ground them up as well. Renewal without the memory that we retained, but they did not, produced only an endlessly accelerating rotation around our own axis. It seemed as if the worst would continue to be replaced by the even worse never-endingly, and when the desire suddenly arose for a sobering blow from without, the Germans came.

Naïve as we were, we thought the Young Communists were different, not us. But didn't we also reproach ourselves for our own indecisive rejection of the past? Then why disown those who followed through consistently, to the end? We thought the Germans were an absolutely external force, intent on destroying our way of life. But did we really like our way of life? And if we had been prepared to block their way immediately and firmly, would they really have got this far and encircled us? We thought the German were "not us" to the power of two.

But it was all us.

April. There is no date or year. Time has stopped.

The music paper has run out, and I have no desire to draw lines on huge sheets of Whatman paper that no one needs any longer. But ironically enough, there is more ink and pencil lead than I could use. And heavy-duty drafting paper too (it simply burned very badly in winter). And in general I am exhausted. But the most important, the final thing, is what has become irrevocably clear as the horror wanes: in the silence, with no air raids or artillery bombardments, with no aching hunger—in my brain. The series of variations that rang out, accompanied by the sirens of the first air raids an eternity ago—in that fantastical autumn—was conceived correctly. What dialectic of I and not-I, of we and not-we, can there be, when the external and the internal are one, when our enemy and our comrade are only the masks of our own fear, self-deception, valor, and shame?

There can be no contrasting themes, no voices with different tones.

And there must be no instruments.

The only active elements are fundamental phenomena and states in their multifarious combinability:

City	Hunger	Snow
River	Sun	Faith
Death	Despondency	Life

Variation I:

Sun	Hunger	Despondency
Snow	Vera	River
Life	City	Death

Variation II:

Despondency	Snow	Sun
Vera	River	Life
Hunger	City	(I don't know)

Variation III:

Death	Despondency	Hunger
Hunger	Despondency	Death
Despondency	Hunger	Despondency

Variation IV:

Vera	(I don't know)	Vera
Despondency	Snow	(I don't know)
Snow	Snow	River

Variation V:

Life	Life	Death
Sun	Sun	Hunger
Hunger	Hunger	Snow

But I know what the title of my life's work—my death's work—is, and for the first time I am not ashamed to utter it. I, who avoided it for eighteen years, hoping for the resurrection of a vibrant, resonant shadow. But that shadow suddenly started devouring the sun, consuming my heart, which has been sucked dry by hunger and poisoned by endless sadness.

The music retreats underground and proliferates in a stifling conflagration, blotting out the visible light.

And so—it is called "Leningrad." Nothing more or less: *Leningrad.*

p. 25   *Amo, et cupio . . .*: "'I love and desire you,' 'you alone are dear to me,' 'without you I cannot live'—and the various other ways in which women express their feelings and arouse passion in others."

p. 32   *Julius Pokorny* (1887–1970): foremost expert on Indo-European etymology and a champion of Celtic and Germanic national and linguistic awareness. Born a Catholic in Prague to a family of Jewish ancestry, he was forced to leave the University of Berlin after the Nazi takeover, and continued his research in Switzerland.

p. 40   *not done to speak of aloud*: Vasilii Beklemishev could have been permitted to go abroad with the understanding that he was continuing "special work" for the Soviet government—not an uncommon practice in the early 1920s. The great Russian Indologist Prince Stcherbatsky (see below) had been asked to visit London in order to lobby his aristocratic contacts, which included Britain's former Viceroy and Governor-General of India, then State Secretary for Foreign Affairs, Lord Curzon.

p. 42   *Lokh* (pl. *lokhi*): in contemporary Russian, the archaic term *lokh* became a slang word for a weak and easily deceived man.

p. 42   *Cathy's Garden*: Cathy's (Catherine's) Garden, *Katen'kin* (*Yekaterininsky*) *sad*, is a relatively small public garden in the very center of the city with a monumental statue of Catherine the Great surrounded by her statesmen, soldiers, poets, and lovers. Alexandrinsky Theater is to the south of the garden; the Yeliseev Grocery Store is to the north; and the former Imperial Public Library (currently the National Library of Russia) is to the west. We can assume that Chetvertinsky has just exited the Public Library and is heading east, toward the Staronevsky part of Nevsky Prospect, where he lives.

p. 49   *Mordovtsev*: Daniil Lukich Mordovtsev (also known as Danylo Mordovets, 1830—1905) was an extremely prolific author of historical fiction and monographic studies of impostors and robbers. Although Mordovtsev (or · Mordovets) considered himself a Ukrainian, grew up among Russian-speaking Don Cossacks, and resided in St. Petersburg and Rostov-on-Don, his last name hints at Finno-Ugric ancestry.

p. 49   *Helsingfors*: the Swedish name for Helsinki was widely in use among Russians when the Grand Duchy of Finland (1809–1917) was a part of the Russian Empire.

p. 50   *Platon Karataev*: a character from Tolstoy's *War and Peace*, an idealized peasant.

p. 51   *the refuge of the wretched Finn*: Line 8 of Alexander Pushkin's poem "The Bronze Horseman: A Petersburg Tale."

p. 55   *Pitinbrukh*: A distorted from of *Piter-Burkh*, the original early eighteenth-century name of St. Petersburg; hence St. Petersburg's popular nickname of "Piter." *Pitinbrukh* appears in various nineteenth-century documents and could be translated as something like "drink and stuff your belly."

p. 60   *Ulla*: cf. H. G. Wells's *The War of the Worlds*: "'Ulla, ulla, ulla, ulla,' wailed that superhuman note—great waves of sound sweeping down the broad, sunlit roadway, between the tall buildings on each side." In early Soviet Russia, H. G. Wells's story of the Martian invasion of Earth was interpreted as a parable of the forthcoming total war between antagonistic civilizations and classes.

p. 73   *Marx*: Adolf Fyodorovich Marx (1838–1904) was a German-born Russian publisher famous for his cheap editions of Russian and world classics.

p. 74   At Tikhon's: a chapter from Dostoyevsky's *The Devils* (also known in English as *The Possessed* and *The Demons*), containing the confessions of metaphysical, political, and moral nihilist Nikolai Stavrogin. It was suppressed on the novel's first publication, and only appeared after its rediscovery in 1922. It is generally appended to *The Devils* in contemporary editions, but has also been published under its own cover. Leonid Petrovich Grossman (1888–1965) was a Russian literary scholar, who specialized in Pushkin and Dostoyevsky.

p. 96   *a working day in the Soviet calendar*: the only official Soviet holidays at the time were Red Army and Navy Day (February 23), International Labor Day (May 1), and the day of the October Revolution (November 7, according to the Gregorian calendar). During the war, everyone worked a seven-day week.

p. 105   *pure alcohol*: each Red Army soldier of the day was entitled to one hundred free grams of vodka per day (it was considered to be a form of stress relief). Still, for civilians, "pure alcohol" was a valuable treat and possession.

p. 106 *fog, mist, smoke*: an untranslatable series of puns. "Tumanov" is a Russified version of an aristocratic Georgian (and Armenian) surname, but is almost identical to the Russian word for fog, mist, etc. Further, the Latin for these same vaporous entities is *nebula*, hence Iraklii's alias of Nebulovich ... and, finally, *ne buló* in Ukrainian means "something that was not."

p. 108 *Prince Stcherbatsky*: Fyodor Ippolitovich Shcherbatskoy (1866–1942), an Indologist who directed the Institute of Buddhist Culture in Leningrad from 1928 to 1930, and was in charge of the Cabinet of Indo-Tibetan Culture of the Institute of Eastern Studies of the Russian Academy of Sciences from 1930 to 1942. Between 1918 and 1932, he published a number of groundbreaking studies—all in English, signing his name "Stcherbatsky"—on dharma, nirvana, and Buddhist logic in general. Until the Siege of Leningrad, Prince Stcherbatsky lived in his apartment by University Embankment on Vasilievsky Island. He was famous for his generosity; one typical story tells that, upon learning that one of his graduate students had become interested in music, he offered her his own grand piano as a gift, claiming that he'd stopped playing it anyway.

Appendix

Historical and Soviet Names of the Streets, Gardens, and Bridges Mentioned in *Leningrad*

Historical Name, dates in use	*Soviet Name, dates in use*
15th Line of Vasilievsky Island, before 1918 and since 1944	Vera Slutskaya Street, 1918–1944
Anichkov Bridge	No name change
Annunciation Bridge, before 1855 and since 2007; Nicolas I Bridge, 1855–1918	Lieutenant Schmidt Bridge, 1918–2007
Annunciation Square, before 1918	Labor Square, since 1918, still in use
Big Neva River Embankment, before 1887; Nicolas I Embankment, 1887–1918	Lieutenant Schmidt Embankment, since 1918, still in use
Catherine's Garden, or, more commonly, Cathy's Garden, before 1923 and since circa 1991	The garden on Ostrovsky Square, 1923–circa 1991
Garden Street, before 1923 and since 1944	July 3 Street, 1923–1944
Greater Prospect of Vasilievsky Island, before 1918 and since 1944	Friedrich Adler Prospect, 1918–1922; Proletarian Victory Prospect, 1922–1944
Horse Guard Boulevard, before 1918 and since 1991	Trade Unions Boulevard, 1918–1991
Ligovskaya Street (or simply Ligovka), before 1956	Ligovsky Prospect, since 1956
Liteiny Prospect, before 1918 and since 1944	Volodarsky Prospect, 1918–1944

Middle Prospect of Vasilievsky Island, before 1939 and since 1944	Mussorgsky Prospect, 1939–1944
Nevsky Prospect, before 1918 and since 1944	October 25 Prospect, 1918–1944
Palace Bridge, before 1918 and since 1952	Bridge of the Republic, 1918–1952
Palace Square, before 1918 and since 1944	Uritsky Square, 1918–1944
Rasstannaya Street	No name change
Staronevsky Prospect, part of Nevsky Prospect between Moscow Station and St. Alexander Nevsky Monastery, before 1918 and since 1944	October 25 Prospect, 1918–1944
Tauride Garden, before 1930 and since 1985	First Five-Year Plan Garden, 1930–1950; Municipal Children's Park, 1950–1985

IGOR GEORGIEVICH VISHNEVETSKY was born in 1964. In 1986 he graduated from the Faculty of Philology at Moscow State University and in 1996 received a PhD in Slavic languages from Brown University. Vishnevetsky has authored six collections of poetry, two monographs—on Andrei Bely and Russian émigré composers of the 1920s and 1930s—and a 700-page biography of Sergei Prokofiev. Although he publishes almost exclusively in Russian, some of his research has been written in English, including two literary biographies—of Andrei Bely and Arsenii Tarkovsky. His poetry and prose has been printed in Russian literary journals, including *Znamya*, *October*, and *Novy Mir*.

ANDREW BROMFIELD is a British editor and translator of Russian literature. He was a founding editor of the journal *Glas*, and has translated into English works by Boris Akunin, Vladimir Voinovich, Irina Denezhkina, Victor Pelevin, Mikhail Shishkin, and Sergei Lukyanenko, among many others.

SELECTED DALKEY ARCHIVE TITLES

SELECTED DALKEY ARCHIVE TITLES

FOR A FULL LIST OF PUBLICATIONS, VISIT:
www.dalkeyarchive.com

JOSEPH MCELROY,
   Night Soul and Other Stories.
ABDELWAHAB MEDDEB, *Talismano.*
GERHARD MEIER, *Isle of the Dead.*
HERMAN MELVILLE, *The Confidence-Man.*
AMANDA MICHALOPOULOU, *I'd Like.*
STEVEN MILLHAUSER, *The Barnum Museum.*
   In the Penny Arcade.
RALPH J. MILLS, JR., *Essays on Poetry.*
MOMUS, *The Book of Jokes.*
CHRISTINE MONTALBETTI, *The Origin of Man.*
   Western.
OLIVE MOORE, *Spleen.*
NICHOLAS MOSLEY, *Accident.*
   Assassins.
   Catastrophe Practice.
   Experience and Religion.
   A Garden of Trees.
   Hopeful Monsters.
   Imago Bird.
   Impossible Object.
   Inventing God.
   Judith.
   Look at the Dark.
   Natalie Natalia.
   Serpent.
   Time at War.
WARREN MOTTE,
   *Fables of the Novel: French Fiction
      since 1990.*
   *Fiction Now: The French Novel in
      the 21st Century.*
   *Oulipo: A Primer of Potential
      Literature.*
GERALD MURNANE, *Barley Patch.*
   Inland.
YVES NAVARRE, *Our Share of Time.*
   Sweet Tooth.
DOROTHY NELSON, *In Night's City.*
   Tar and Feathers.
ESHKOL NEVO, *Homesick.*
WILFRIDO D. NOLLEDO, *But for the Lovers.*
FLANN O'BRIEN, *At Swim-Two-Birds.*
   The Best of Myles.
   The Dalkey Archive.
   The Hard Life.
   The Poor Mouth.
   The Third Policeman.
CLAUDE OLLIER, *The Mise-en-Scène.*
   Wert and the Life Without End.
GIOVANNI ORELLI, *Walaschek's Dream.*
PATRIK OUŘEDNÍK, *Europeana.*
   The Opportune Moment, 1855.
BORIS PAHOR, *Necropolis.*
FERNANDO DEL PASO, *News from the
      Empire.*
   Palinuro of Mexico.
ROBERT PINGET, *The Inquisitory.*
   Mahu or The Material.
   Trio.
MANUEL PUIG, *Betrayed by Rita Hayworth.*

The Buenos Aires Affair.
Heartbreak Tango.
RAYMOND QUENEAU, *The Last Days.*
   Odile.
   Pierrot Mon Ami.
   Saint Glinglin.
ANN QUIN, *Berg.*
   Passages.
   Three.
   Tripticks.
ISHMAEL REED, *The Free-Lance Pallbearers.*
   The Last Days of Louisiana Red.
   Ishmael Reed: The Plays.
   Juice!
   Reckless Eyeballing.
   The Terrible Threes.
   The Terrible Twos.
   Yellow Back Radio Broke-Down.
JASIA REICHARDT, *15 Journeys Warsaw
      to London.*
NOËLLE REVAZ, *With the Animals.*
JOÃO UBALDO RIBEIRO, *House of the
      Fortunate Buddhas.*
JEAN RICARDOU, *Place Names.*
RAINER MARIA RILKE, *The Notebooks of
      Malte Laurids Brigge.*
JULIÁN RÍOS, *The House of Ulysses.*
   Larva: A Midsummer Night's Babel.
   Poundemonium.
   Procession of Shadows.
AUGUSTO ROA BASTOS, *I the Supreme.*
DANIËL ROBBERECHTS, *Arriving in Avignon.*
JEAN ROLIN, *The Explosion of the
      Radiator Hose.*
OLIVIER ROLIN, *Hotel Crystal.*
ALIX CLEO ROUBAUD, *Alix's Journal.*
JACQUES ROUBAUD, *The Form of a
      City Changes Faster, Alas, Than
      the Human Heart.*
   The Great Fire of London.
   Hortense in Exile.
   Hortense Is Abducted.
   The Loop.
   Mathematics:
   The Plurality of Worlds of Lewis.
   The Princess Hoppy.
   Some Thing Black.
RAYMOND ROUSSEL, *Impressions of Africa.*
VEDRANA RUDAN, *Night.*
STIG SÆTERBAKKEN, *Siamese.*
   Self Control.
LYDIE SALVAYRE, *The Company of Ghosts.*
   The Lecture.
   The Power of Flies.
LUIS RAFAEL SÁNCHEZ,
   Macho Camacho's Beat.
SEVERO SARDUY, *Cobra & Maitreya.*
NATHALIE SARRAUTE,
   Do You Hear Them?
   Martereau.
   The Planetarium.

FOR A FULL LIST OF PUBLICATIONS, VISIT:
www.dalkeyarchive.com